THE FAVOR

A JAMES THOMAS NOVELLA

BROOKE SIVENDRA

1

JAMES THOMAS

He drew a short breath, his body reacting on instinct. He pulled his pistol, keeping it low underneath the table, his finger steady on the trigger. His heart pounded against his rib cage, threatening to lurch through his chest as his eyes tracked the man who was no more than ten paces ahead. A man who'd just walked straight past James while he'd been eating his dinner.

James threw a few bills down on the table—enough to cover his meal—and moved toward the wall. He drew his cell phone, his eyes never leaving the man whose head was roaming in an arc—a mannerism James knew well.

He was looking for something.

Or, more likely, someone.

The call connected. "Brother," James said in a hushed voice, "is Nicole with you?"

"Yes. Why? What's going on?" Deacon asked, quickly.

"Go home now. Lock the doors and watch the security screens."

"Where are you?" Deacon's voice heightened.

"Downtown. I've seen an old friend . . ." James said.

"Who?" Deacon asked, his voice now full of tension.

It was hard to hear his brother above the bustling noise of

animated talking, but there was one advantage to an overpopulated street—it was easier to hide.

"Timothy Tanaka." James stepped sideways, away from the crimson lights and into the shadows. "I'll meet you at home."

He hung up the phone, craning his neck, doing a full surveillance of his environment. He couldn't see any men following Tanaka, but that didn't surprise James—assassins didn't often travel in groups. They preferred going solo; at least, James always had.

The side street was crammed as James veered into the human traffic. His head brushed against the hanging lanterns as he kept his back as close to the vendor stalls as possible. James's eyes left the man only to look for any friends he might have in tow.

What is Tanaka doing in Tokyo?

James's eyes darted up, surveying the windows above, but there were too many blinking lights to get a proper look.

His finger stayed steady on the trigger, alert and poised as he watched.

James didn't have the answer, but, by the way his stomach was curdling, he made an assumption—the CIA had sent him to eliminate a target. A target named Liam Smith, or, as he now liked to call himself, James Thomas.

James took a steeling breath.

Breathe. Focus.

He wove through the crowd, keeping a distance from Tanaka that allowed him to keep his eyes on him but not alert him to his presence. Tanaka walked casually, his shoulders low and loose. His hands swung by his sides, but James didn't need X-ray vision to know at least one pistol was hidden underneath his jacket. Nothing about Tanaka's body language told James the man was on high alert, though —high alert for an assassin, that was. Their minds worked on a different level; they were always watching, always sensitive to their environments. The average person on the street wouldn't be able to tell you where the next lane exit was, which rooftop would be easiest to scale, if there were any police in the street. But James could. And he knew Tanaka could, too.

Tanaka stopped and James ducked behind a group of men. One of them eyeballed James but he gave him a dismissive nod, one that indicated he should go back to his conversation and pay no attention to James.

Tanaka entered a stall and struck up a conversation with the woman behind the grill. She laughed at something he said, completely oblivious to the danger of the man she was serving.

He was lethal.

James looked over his shoulder, surveying his environment again. He took two steps sideways, checking the angle, but there were too many people in the bustling street to get a clear shot.

And James wasn't convinced a clear shot was a good idea anyway.

They—James, Deacon, and Nicole—had been careful since they'd left Russia. Extremely careful, and James didn't believe the CIA had solid evidence that they were in Tokyo, or that Nicole was even with them. And that meant they'd sent Tanaka here on a hunch. And if something happened to Tanaka—if the man didn't report in—they'd send another agent or multiple agents. And then James, Deacon, and Nicole would have to start over.

Again.

James could do it; he'd done it his whole life. But Deacon and Nicole were different. They needed stability, they wanted a normal life—as much as they could have one.

Play it safe, James told himself. *Watch and wait.*

2

KYOJI TOHMATSU

Kyoji eyeballed his opponent across the table from him, the corner of his lip turning up. He was as arrogant as he was confident, but Kyoji held the winning hand.

"Make your move and make it fast, Haruto. I've got work to do," Kyoji said, his gaze flickering to the screens to his right. The club was filling up, and that meant he had men to watch and women to schmooze.

Haruto pushed two stacks of chips into the center of the table. He was betting everything he had. *Silly bastard.* Haruto laid down his cards and Kyoji let his full smile bloom. Haruto knew he'd lost before he'd even seen Kyoji's cards.

"Anata ni fakku!" Haruto said, narrowing his eyes. "Anata wa damasareta."

"Go fuck yourself," Kyoji said, chuckling. "And, no, I didn't cheat. When you play with the king, you get burned."

Kyoji made a show of collecting up the chips. "I'll add it to your tab. At the rate you're going, you'll be buying me a new apartment next month."

Haruto snorted and waved his hand dismissively.

The door to Kyoji's office opened, and his eyes landed on a

lingerie-clad girl by the name of Rebecca. And she was a girl, not even old enough to legally work in the adult club, but Kyoji had hired her anyway because she was beautiful, intelligent, and had a work ethic he appreciated. She was good for business and brought in more money with her clothes on than some of the woman who took theirs off.

"Kyoji, there's a man at the bar asking for you," she said, hesitantly.

"Who is he?" Kyoji asked.

She shook her head. "I'm not sure—I've never seen him before. I don't think he's from around here." She walked toward the computer screen and pointed at a figure. "There. That's him."

Kyoji enlarged the image, noting the man was looking directly at the camera.

Interesting.

Kyoji nodded. "I'll be out in a minute," he said but his eyes didn't leave the screen as he continued to watch the man. He had one hand on a glass that he turned with his fingertips but didn't actually drink from, and the other hand was laid casually on the bar. Kyoji took it as a message that he wasn't planning to cause trouble.

He retrieved a pistol from the top drawer of his desk and nodded to Haruto who slid his chair back, following behind him.

Kyoji took a moment to look over the club. Without the door numbers it was a guess, but he thought they were over capacity and the night was just beginning.

I need additional locations, Kyoji thought. It was time to expand yet again.

As Kyoji approached the bar, the patrons moved, creating a space for him.

"I hear you're looking for me," he said, turning his gaze to the man sitting at the bar.

The man dipped his head subtly. "I am. I've heard you're the guy who might be able to help me. I'm looking for an old friend," the man said with an American accent.

Kyoji raised an eyebrow. This was *very* interesting. "What is your name?"

"Tim."

"Well, Tim, why don't you come with me and we'll have a chat," Kyoji said. "And bring that drink you're using as a prop."

Tim gave a crooked smile and stood.

Kyoji looked over his shoulder, spotting Haruto and the boys close by. He nodded toward the VIP area before moving toward it with Tim at his side.

Kyoji ordered a waitress to clear out a booth, one that was positioned directly behind the glass wall looking out onto the stage. If the men were going to talk, they might as well have a good view.

"Take a seat," Kyoji said, gesturing toward the couch.

Kyoji sat, too, lighting a cigarette and then offering one to his guest. Tim shook his head and Kyoji threw the packet on the table in front of them. He drew in a long breath, analyzing the man sitting in front of him.

"So, who's your long-lost friend?" Kyoji asked.

Tim pulled out his phone, typed on the screen and then turned it to show Kyoji.

A glorified mug shot. A face with no name.

Kyoji knew Tim was watching him, analyzing his reaction. But Kyoji didn't react. He'd never seen the man before.

Kyoji shrugged. "Why did you think I'd know him?"

"Because I've been told Tokyo is your playground. I'd be surprised if someone was doing contract work on your turf, and you didn't know about it," Tim said, seeming to choose his words carefully.

Contract work. Kyoji honestly had never seen the man, but now he had an idea who he was.

"Well, I'm flattered that someone is speaking so highly of me," Kyoji said with a grin. "But, I don't know the man. If he's doing contract work, he's not doing it for us, nor is he doing it for our rivals. I focus my attention where it needs to be, not across all of Tokyo. If it doesn't concern us, I don't need to know about it. I wish I could help you, but I don't recognize the man."

Tim tilted his head, looked thoughtful for a moment, and then he appeared to accept Kyoji's words. He passed him a card. "If you see him, give me a call."

Kyoji looked at the white card. It was blank except for a phone number.

Kyoji sucked in a long drag of his cigarette before responding. "Perhaps I'll just tell him you're looking for him . . . less hassle that way, and then you can take it off my turf and spill blood elsewhere." Kyoji's low voice sent a clear message.

Their eyes locked.

"Just give me a call," Tim said before moving toward the door.

Koji nodded at security to escort him out.

He finished his cigarette, looking out over the stage, but he wasn't really watching. He was thinking. He didn't like the situation. And he didn't like outsiders hunting each other in his city—it brought trouble.

Kyoji went back into his office, poured himself a drink, and sat quietly for a moment. And then he dialed his uncle, the leader of the Tohmatsu clan.

"Konnichiwa," Haruki said, greeting him.

"Konnichiwa. What do you know about the guy who's doing contract work for that dirty grub, Saito?"

"Little other than he's very good. Or, *they* are very good. He has a brother, apparently—they do Saito's detail together. God only knows why he needs two of them for protection . . . that politician has made one too many dirty deals. Why do you ask?"

"Someone's looking for him. At least I think it's him. Have you seen his face?"

"Negative. I'm not sure I like the sound of this, son."

"I don't like it either," Kyoji said without hesitation, chewing on his bottom lip, strategizing how best to go about this. "I'll make a few inquiries," Kyoji added before ending the call.

He mentally ran through Saito's known contacts, wondering who might've seen him, and who was likely to talk.

Perhaps a female friend, Kyoji thought. Saito was known for buying sex, and Kyoji didn't think his security detail would let him engage in such acts without screening the prostitutes first. There was one tall, leggy Swedish woman who was Saito's favorite, and she happened to be an old friend of Kyoji's.

He dialed her number.

3

JAMES THOMAS

James quickened his pace as light replaced darkness. Luckily for him, gangsters didn't comply with legal closing times, and Kyoji Tohmatsu's club was still pumping. Patrons were stumbling out, and James had no doubt their pockets were empty and Kyoji's were full.

James crossed the street, aware that the bouncer was looking him up and down. "The club's closed, sir. We open again at ten p.m."

"I'm here to see Kyoji," James said, noting the tattoos on the man's hands. He was part of the Tohmatsu gang as James expected. Who else would Kyoji have guarding his club?

"You're not on my list," the bouncer said, without asking for a name or looking at a list.

"Tell him James Thomas is here to see him."

Their eyes locked and seconds passed. Finally the man put a finger to his ear and James knew he'd just activated his earpiece.

"There's a James Thomas here to see Kyoji . . . Okay."

The bouncer's eyes narrowed at James. "Weapon," he said.

James placed his pistol in the man's open palm. "Don't lose that; I'm quite attached to it," James said as the door opened and he stepped inside.

The music reverberated beneath his feet and a woman appeared in front of him, dazzling him with a million-dollar smile—although James doubted that was the first thing most of the men noticed given that she wore only a sheer lace bra.

"This way," she whispered in his ear.

James followed her, his senses heightened. He could be walking into a dragon's lair but James knew one thing about Kyoji—he kept the violent underground dealings out of his club during operating hours. More than likely, they happened in the dark lane that ran along the rear of the property. If James ended up out there then he knew he had to worry.

Despite the round, perky ass swaying in front of him, James kept his mind focused as they took the stairs, walked the length of second level, and stopped at a black door. The woman opened it, holding it aside for James.

It was quiet inside and his eyes landed on Kyoji immediately, who was puffing on a cigarette. Their eyes met, and with a single look the woman disappeared as James approached the couch where Kyoji was seated. There were six other men lining the walls of the room—bodyguards. James sat only when motioned to.

"So, you're James Thomas, I assume," Kyoji said, rubbing his chin.

"I am. Thank you for meeting me," James said.

"Oh, the pleasure is all mine, but I can't imagine why the fuck you're here," Kyoji said, his teeth bared in an aggressive smile.

James raised one eyebrow. "I think you know exactly why I'm here. I'd like to know the details of your meeting with Timothy Tanaka a few hours ago."

Kyoji's eyes narrowed. "What makes you think I know, or met with, a Timothy Tanaka?"

James smirked. "Because I was watching you." He looked over the room. "How come I'm not getting the VIP treatment?"

Kyoji stilled. "How the fuck did you get into, and out of, my club unseen?"

James knew after Tanaka's visit Kyoji would've put his security on high alert.

"You've got a weak spot in your security system," he said casually.

"I came in through the second-floor window. I'll show you before I leave so that you can rectify it . . . if you tell me what I want to know."

Kyoji leaned forward. "You're bribing me in my own club?"

James didn't lean back; he didn't react to Kyoji at all. He would not let anyone intimidate him. "I'm offering you a gift," James said. "In fact, I'd also make a few other improvements if it were my club, but then I'm very obsessive about such details. What did Tanaka want?"

Kyoji eyeballed him before he took another long, slow drag of his cigarette—he wasn't going to be rushed by James, or likely anyone else. "I think you already know what he wants."

"Why did he come here?"

"He said he'd been told I was the man about town that knew things . . . like a name to match a face, that kind of thing."

"And you told him?" James's chest constricted—Kyoji's answer could change everything.

"Actually, I didn't," Kyoji said.

Relief washed over him, but James ensured his face remained impassive.

Kyoji continued. "I wasn't entirely sure who you were until about an hour ago. It's funny who will talk, given the right price."

"Everyone has a price," James agreed. He wanted to ask Kyoji who had told him, but not only did he think Kyoji wouldn't divulge the source, he didn't want Kyoji to know it worried him.

Kyoji searched his eyes, blowing out a ring of smoke. "Let me say this once . . . in good faith . . . Tanaka, as you call him, showed me a picture and asked if I knew who you were. I didn't know, although I had an idea given the things I'd heard about Saito's new security," Kyoji said. "Tanaka gave me his number and told me to call if anything came up. That is it, and that is where it ends. Whatever shit you're in, you keep it out of my club and off of my streets. Understood?"

For the first time tonight James saw why Kyoji had earned the reputation he had. The look in his eyes was one James unfortunately knew all too well.

"You have my word . . . I'll kill him on your rival's turf instead," James said, smugly.

Kyoji held his gaze then threw his head back, laughing. "Who are you?" he eventually asked, seemingly more to himself than to James. "Do you want his number to help you accomplish that?"

James grinned. "No thanks, I don't need it. I know where he's sleeping. I even know what bed he's in." He stood to leave. Deacon was watching that room now and James was eager to get back—he didn't know how long Tanaka would nap. "Thank you for your time."

"Whoa," Kyoji said, shaking his head, and James heard the familiar sound of guns being cocked.

His eyes darted around the room. The odds weren't good if he were to try anything.

Kyoji continued, "Don't you dare think you're walking out of here right now. Show me the security leaks."

"I'll show you how I got in," James said. "But right now I'm a bit of a hurry. Give me some time to clean up my business, and I'll come back and do a full assessment of your club and redesign your security —on the house."

Kyoji's gaze locked with James's. "You might be dead before nightfall, and then I won't get my security upgrade."

"If your men don't lower your weapons and let me out of here as soon as possible, there's a much higher chance I'll be dead by nightfall," James said with hard eyes.

Kyoji tapped his finger on his lips. "Show me how you got in. And then be back here within forty-eight hours—not a minute later."

James hated answering to anyone, but right now he was playing Kyoji's game. They'd kept a low profile in Tokyo, careful to stay under the radar of its two infamous gangs, and pissing Kyoji Tohmatsu off was a very bad idea.

"You've got a deal," James said, his voice neutral.

"Who does Tanaka work for?" Kyoji's eyes sparkled like he'd just won a game of chess.

James knew the question wasn't about Tanaka—it was about James. It was a way for Kyoji to glean information. James could lie—

he was a good liar—but if Kyoji found out later, things would get ugly.

"The CIA," James answered, and Kyoji's lips spread into a thin smile.

"Well, well, well," Kyoji said, seemingly pleased with himself. He gave a slight shrug of his shoulders, picked up his cigarettes and glass of whiskey, and stood.

"Lead the way, Thomas," Kyoji said, tilting his head toward the door.

James set a fast pace, eager to get this over with and to get back to his brother. Nicole was locked in their safe house so at least they didn't have to worry about her for the time being.

James looked at his watch, calculating how quickly he could get across town to the hotel where Tanaka was staying. One hour, he concluded.

Deacon was perched on the rooftop, looking through the lens of a sniper rifle when James arrived.

"Any movement?" James asked, crouching beside his brother.

Deacon shook his head. "He's still inside."

Tanaka was staying in the Tivoli hotel—a hotel that had certain rules that were never broken, not even by James. While Tanaka was inside that building they couldn't touch him even if they wanted to—and James wasn't sure he did.

James positioned himself against the wall while Deacon kept watch.

"How did it go?" Deacon asked, his eye never leaving the lens.

"As good as it could've," James said. He didn't end up in the back alley—that was good. "Tanaka's looking for a name to match my face, which leads me to believe the CIA doesn't have concrete evidence that I'm here. They're desperate; perhaps they heard a whisper of some kind and thought it was worth following up on."

"We're assuming he's working for the CIA . . . that could be a mistake. Maybe he's gone rogue just like we did," Deacon said.

"It's possible," James said. "We need intel, and I'm hesitant to touch Tanaka until we have that. If he disappears, whoever he's working for will send more men. The last place we want a war in is Tokyo. Kyoji Tohmatsu has already warned me to keep it off his streets."

Deacon blew out a frustrated breath. "You want to leave, don't you?"

James heard it in his voice—the words his brother didn't say.

"Not yet," James said.

If James had been on his own he would've fled this morning. There was a market for the kind of work they did—underground contract work—in every city, in every country. They could run forever and not run out of places to hide. But he wasn't alone anymore. For the first time in James's life he had others to consider, and he already knew what they wanted.

James continued. "I think we watch Tanaka until he leaves. We take note of where he goes and who he's talking to. And then we find another way to get intel."

But how? That was the question James had been turning over in his mind all morning. Without interrogating Tanaka, they didn't have another lead.

There were a few things James missed about the CIA, but there was one he missed more than anything—intelligence experts: a glorified name the CIA gave their computer hackers. James had worked with one of the best—the best—shortly before everything went sour, but James hadn't had any contact with the man since he'd walked away from his role as an agent. And no contact with the hacker was a good thing, because if someone could trace their location, it was him.

James wondered again if the man had been the one to give Tanaka the lead. James shook his head—it didn't matter. James, Deacon, and Nicole were on their own now. They, and they alone, were responsible for their survival, and they'd been running since they'd left Russia. Deacon and Nicole needed a break—they needed to be in one place for longer than a few months. James couldn't hold that against them—it was a human desire . . . just one that James didn't possess.

Watch and wait. Take things one hour at a time.

Watch and wait they did, for the next two days. It was excruciatingly boring—although, in their world, boring was good. Tanaka visited several prominent members of the underground, even paying Kyoji Tohmatsu another visit. One James hoped Kyoji would elaborate on tonight when he was due to conduct the security assessment.

Tanaka had boarded a flight to Paris three hours ago, and James didn't know what to make of. What was he doing in Paris? Was he based there? Was he connecting through? James could chase him all over the world, but it wouldn't be productive. A more productive idea was forming in James's mind, and he'd been turning it over relentlessly, looking for holes in it and brainstorming solutions.

The main problem with the idea was that it wasn't something they could do alone—they needed someone without connections to the CIA. Someone that would be crazy enough to do it. James could think of only a few people, and he didn't expect any of them to help them. Why would they?

James heard the apartment door open, followed by voices and the smell of takeout. His stomach groaned in response.

"We got your favorite," Nicole called out from the hallway. They never had guests—never—but even if they were to, Nicole's Russian-tinged American accent would be easy to identify. When she walked in she beamed a smile that made James feel guilty. She had never been anything but nice to James, and she had supported every decision he and Deacon had made. She was a good person, but she wasn't right for their world. A girlfriend was a liability—it made Deacon vulnerable to their enemies.

James had very strong convictions on the lives they should lead in order to survive, and Deacon defied more than one of them. On the matter of Deacon and Nicole's relationship, they'd agreed to disagree. Sometimes, though, when James looked at Deacon and saw his eyes shining, James wondered if Deacon was right: it would all be okay, and no one would get hurt. But then, Deacon hadn't seen the same things James had, and all delusion would vanish from James's mind. It was a cold attitude, but James was cold. That's why he was still alive.

Being in a relationship was not a good idea, but James could say it to Deacon until he was blue in the face and it wouldn't make a difference. The man was in love, and he seemed incapable of letting Nicole go.

"I even got you some dessert," she said, holding up a small bag of Japanese candy.

James forced himself to smile and thank her. He didn't want to be an asshole, and it wasn't her fault, or even Deacon's, that they didn't fully comprehend the danger they were putting themselves in. Some days James wished he hadn't seen the ugliest sides of life.

"Thanks, I appreciate it," James said, pouring three glasses of water and sitting down at their tiny kitchen table. Everything in their Tokyo apartment was tiny. James's feet extended past his bed, but he wasn't complaining—he'd definitely slept in worse places. The apartment was crowded when all three of them were home, but that was rarely the case as usually either Deacon or James was with Saito, providing twenty-four-hour protection for him. This week, however, he was holed up at his estate north of Tokyo. While he was there he didn't need their protection, so that gave them one week to dedicate one hundred percent of their time to sorting out this mess. And it also meant they had to take action—fast.

"You're quiet," Deacon said before he loaded a forkful of noodles into his mouth.

"Thinking. I've got an idea on how to fix this . . ."

James's eyes darted to Nicole. Deacon wasn't going to like it, and Nicole was going to hate it. It would involve them being out of town with her holed up in the safe house, and it would put Deacon in a dangerous position—something she hadn't yet learned how to deal with, but something she was going to have to get used to, given their situation. They didn't live normal lives, and they never would. They would have to watch over their shoulders forever.

Nicole raised her eyes to meet James's as she collected her long, dark hair over one shoulder, twirling it between her fingers—a nervous trait.

"Spit it out," Deacon said.

James gave a tight sigh and rested his fork on his plate. "We go back to Russia. There's a CIA contact there that I think will help us— or at least she could be persuaded to. She has high access, and she'll be able to find out who sent Tanaka. We can go from there."

Deacon's mouth hung open. "If we go back to Russia we're as good as dead."

Nicole's eyes darted between the men who now called themselves brothers. *Brothers*. A front they'd decided on before they proposed their services to Saito. It meant fewer questions about their partnership and how they knew each other, and fewer questions were always good.

"Yes and no . . ." James said. "I'm thinking we'll contract someone else, someone unsuspecting, someone who has no ties to the Russians or the CIA. He can kidnap Angela, then I'll convince her not to talk. We'll slip in and out like ghosts."

"Kidnap? Oh damn. And who do you think we're going to use for that job? We don't exactly have a lot of friends right now," Deacon said, raising an eyebrow.

"That part I don't have a solution for just yet . . . I need to do some more research." James's response was elusive—even though he already had a favorite in mind.

"Where are we going to get the money from?" Nicole asked—a fair question given she was their bookkeeper.

The brothers were earning good money now, but they'd walked away from their lives with nothing more than a few hundred dollars in cash. It took time to build wealth—especially the considerable type of wealth it took to bribe criminals.

"I wasn't thinking of using money," James said. "We'll offer them services of some sort—an open-ended favor."

Deacon rubbed his hands over his face. "This could be a very bad idea."

"True," James said. "But do you have a better one?"

"No," Deacon admitted with faraway eyes.

James wondered where his mind had taken him. Deacon had found himself living a life he'd never wanted—a life he didn't deserve. James had asked himself more than once if some part of Deacon, deep in the recesses of his mind, blamed James for the situation he was in. The failed mission hadn't been James's fault, but James had selected Deacon's team. He'd had hundreds of men to choose from, and he'd chosen Deacon. Deacon's life had been ripped away from him, and now he'd spend his new life in hiding until the day he died.

Everyone ate silently now. James shoveled down the food, eager to get out of the tension that had consumed the apartment like a misty fog.

When he was done, he excused himself, put his dishes in the dishwasher and went to pack his kit.

Deacon came to stand at the doorway. "Are you sure you don't want me to come with you tonight?"

"No, it's okay," James said, wanting to give Deacon the night off. If the next week turned out like he thought it was going to, James wanted Deacon to have at least one night home with his girlfriend. If nothing else, James knew Deacon would be in a better state of mind if he did.

James continued, "But keep your phone on you. There's a good chance Kyoji will want this done tonight, and I'm not going to refuse him. We might need to do a full fit-out tomorrow, starting at five in the morning or whenever he closes the club. I'll let you know."

Deacon nodded. "Just give me a call. Be careful, James."

"I will," James said, patting Deacon's shoulder as he turned to leave. It was as close as the brothers got to a hug.

4

JAMES THOMAS

The club was just opening as James arrived. That would give him about seven hours to redesign the security system, source what he needed and be ready for the install when the club closed.

Kyoji was standing at the door, talking with security, when James arrived.

"I see you're still alive," Kyoji said, grinning.

James returned the grin. "I told you I'd be here. I always keep my word," James said before turning to greet the bouncer. He looked as excited to see James as he had a few nights ago.

"I appreciate that," Kyoji said. "Most fuckers don't. Come on in, Thomas, you've got work to do." Kyoji chuckled and this time James refrained from grimacing. He hated owing people favors, but it was a necessary evil in their world.

The bouncer put a hand out, stopping him. "Bag," he said.

James slung it off his shoulder, unzipped it and let the security guy have a good search through it. James looked up at Kyoji, who watched on with gleeful eyes. Kyoji enjoyed having the upper hand— at least in the present moment. From what James had heard and learned, and from the little he'd seen, Kyoji rarely thought of long-term consequences.

"He's just doing his job," Kyoji said playfully.

With the search complete, James followed Kyoji inside to a room that James had never seen before. An office.

"Take a seat," Kyoji said as he walked toward the private bar. He poured two glasses of whiskey and placed one in front of James before sitting in his chair, one that was so big it looked like a throne. He lit a cigarette and threw the packet toward James.

James didn't want the drink, but he wouldn't say no to a cigarette tonight. He lit one, mindful that his back was to the door. His ears were pricked—it was rare that anyone ever sneaked up on him. And he didn't get the sense that he was in any danger tonight, but he could never afford to be careless.

"So, what happened to your friend?" Kyoji asked.

"Nothing much," James said with a shrug. "He boarded a flight to Paris this afternoon."

"Why'd you let him go?"

"I'm not trying to draw attention to myself," James said, his lungs burning in a pleasurable kind of way—it was the reason he didn't mind the occasional cigarette.

"He came by again. But then you already know that, don't you?"

James opened his mouth to respond, but Kyoji's cell phone rang. Kyoji answered the call, without greeting, and said only two words: "Finish it."

Kyoji returned his attention to James like nothing had happened and gave him an expectant look.

James answered, continuing their conversation, "I do know that. I'd like to know why he came back, and what he wanted."

"I think it was a last-ditch effort," Kyoji said. "Apparently no one knows much about you, which I believe, because I've barely been able to find out anything myself. He did say something very interesting, though . . ." Kyoji paused, teasing.

"Pray tell," James said.

"He called you by another name: Liam Smith. So, are you James Thomas, or are you Liam Smith? Or are you another name completely?" Kyoji had that daring look in his eyes again.

James smirked. "I'm whoever you want me to be. I do prefer James Thomas, though."

Their conversation was yet again interrupted by Kyoji's cell phone. This time the conversation was very different.

"Hey . . . No, I'm just in a meeting . . . Yeah, exactly . . . What time? Okay, see you then."

He hung up the phone. "My kid brother," Kyoji said by way of explanation, and James saw a spark in Kyoji's eyes he hadn't witnessed before now.

James assumed he was referring to Jayce Tohmatsu. The prodigy stepson of the billionaire, Sr. Tohmatsu—the gangster turned successful, legitimate businessman. It was the makeover story of the century, and one James had found fascinating while doing his research on Tokyo.

Clearly, though, that reformation hadn't extended to the rest of the Tohmatsu line.

"Anyway—it's been lovely chatting, but you have some work to do," Kyoji said. "I want you to start in this office and work through every single room. I'll have someone assist you, obviously. I can't just let you roam around my club unattended."

"But you trust me to set up a new security system for you?" James asked.

"I don't know yet, but I'm interested to find out what you come up with. Let's see what you're made of, and we'll go from there."

James nodded, took one last drag of his cigarette before butting it in the overflowing ashtray on Kyoji's desk, and got straight to business. "I need to see the club when it's empty, too. I'll do what I can tonight, put the basics together, but I'll need more time in the morning."

Kyoji smirked. "I don't give a fuck if you sleep here for the next two nights. Get to work, agent boy."

◈

James, with the company of one of Kyoji's staff, spent the rest of the night analyzing the current security plan then redesigning a new one. As he exited the room he'd first spoken with Kyoji in, James saw the man below, his arm slung over the shoulders of Jayce Tohmatsu. Jayce looked younger in person, and James mentally calculated his age given what he'd read in the papers. Twenty-one, maybe twenty-two. And already the Vice President of Tohmatsu Limited.

Jayce said something and Kyoji howled with laughter, slapping him on the back. The braless women around them giggled. Kyoji lived in another world—one James would never be a part of.

But, as playful and carefree as Kyoji appeared, when their eyes met James knew otherwise. Kyoji had been discretely watching him all night—he knew every room James was walking in and out of in real time.

From the time James had arrived in Tokyo, he'd made it his business to learn about everyone in the underground world—especially the most powerful men. Kyoji was second only to his uncle, Haruki Tohmatsu. Kyoji was even more powerful than their rival's leader and he'd earned a reputation of being *fair*. James almost smiled to himself. *Fair*, in gang terms, meant that those who were loyal were rewarded. Those that were not ended up begging for Satan to take them.

The rest of the night passed quickly, and when the music turned off James crawled out of the ceiling, dropping onto his feet, light like a cat. He brushed the dust off his clothing.

"How's it looking?" Kyoji said, walking in.

"It's a good system," James admitted, stifling a yawn.

"But?"

James shrugged. "But it wouldn't keep a guy like me or Tanaka out."

Kyoji jaw jutted out. "Come with me."

Kyoji left the room without another word, and James picked up his kit, striding fast to keep up with Kyoji. They went back to Kyoji's office.

"Start talking," Kyoji said the moment he closed the door.

"Like I said, I need to review some aspects with proper lighting, but these are your major problems areas," James began, pulling out his sketchbook.

For the next hour James detailed the system he would install, counteracting the issues he'd identified.

"I assume you learned this in the CIA?" Kyoji asked.

"Some of it, yes. Some of it was learned through necessity," James said, leaning back in his chair. After a second night with barely any sleep, his eyes felt like they were coated in gritty sand.

"You're a man of mysteries, aren't you?" Kyoji asked with gleaming eyes. "What'll this cost? You don't look like a cheap guy."

James scoffed. "I'll take that as a compliment. But I'll do this one on the house—a thank you for not ratting me out to Tanaka."

If Kyoji had revealed his identity, they wouldn't be having this conversation tonight. They wouldn't even be in the same building. James would've killed Tanaka, and then he would've come for Kyoji, before fleeing Tokyo.

"I don't have a single fucking reason in the world to trust you to install this system," Kyoji said, leaning forward on his elbows.

"And you don't have one not to, either," James said, raising one eyebrow. "Do you think I'm foolish enough not to do my research? I know exactly who you are, Kyoji Tohmatsu, and I know exactly what you're capable of. I've done nothing but keep a low profile since I came here. If I were looking for trouble, you would've seen it by now. Besides, when do we really know who to trust? Trust is a very dangerous game."

Silence hung in the air as Kyoji chewed his cheek. "When can you do it?"

James looked to the security screens. The club was almost empty. "I can start now. I'll finalize the plan, source the items I need, and then I'll do the install with my brother. I don't want any of your guys involved—it'll just waste time."

"I do like efficiency," Kyoji said as he held out his hand, and James made the deal.

With the lights on, James worked fast, finalizing the security plan.

"Hey," James said, answering his phone.

"How's it going?" Deacon asked.

"Good, I'm almost done. I'm going to send you a list of stuff we need. Can you source what we don't already have and meet me at the club?" James asked, balancing his phone between his shoulder and one ear as he pulled out some existing wiring.

"Yeah, sure," Deacon said, but the sound of glass shattering stole James's attention.

"Hang on, I'll call you back," James whispered before ending the call. He moved toward the door, his feet silent on the carpet, inching toward the railing, grateful the lights were still off.

From the balcony, he had a front row seat to the scene below.

Kyoji was perched on a bar stool with a broken glass in his hands. Its razor-sharp shards were pressed against a man's neck.

The floor around their feet glimmered as tiny fragments of glass reflected the overhead lights.

"Anata wa bakadesu," Kyoji said with a hoarse voice.

James's Japanese was still a work in progress, but he understood well enough: *You're a fool.*

"Watashi ga kidzukanai to omoimashita ka?" Kyoji growled.

Did you think I wouldn't notice?

The man stuttered, pleading.

Kyoji rammed the glass into the man's neck and his eyes bulged as red streaks trickled down his throat.

James's eyes darted around the room. None of Kyoji's men looked surprised, nor did they look sickened by what they'd just witnessed.

The man fell off the stool, drawing his last breaths.

Kyoji crouched down, whispering in his ear. James couldn't help but wonder what he was saying.

Kyoji stood, moving in the direction of his office. "Clean up the fucking mess!" he yelled over his shoulder.

James slinked back into the shadows and went back to work.

Deacon: I'm out front.

James crawled out from the ceiling once more—he'd be grateful when this job was done.

On his way to meet his brother, he looked down at the bar but couldn't see a trace of evidence of the crime that had been committed earlier. The boys knew how to clean up well.

At the front door, Deacon was getting the same treatment from the bouncer that James had become accustomed to.

"He's with me. You can check with Kyoji," James said. It was an effort to keep his voice neutral—sleep deprivation was shortening his normally long fuse.

The bouncer did the check, then James led him toward Kyoji's office.

James knocked twice and pressed his ear to the door.

"Come in."

James entered first. "Kyoji, meet my brother, Deacon Thomas."

Kyoji's eyes darted between the men. "Interesting," was all he said.

James kept his face neutral—that word could mean so many things. "We'll start on the upper levels and work down. We'll let you know if we need anything."

Kyoji gave a small nod. James wondered if the dark circles under his own eyes matched Kyoji's.

"He's friendly," Deacon whispered once they were out of hearing range.

"He's had a rough night," James said, arching a brow. He'd fill his brother in on the details later. "The sooner we get this done the better."

The brothers worked relentlessly, crawling into and out of spaces, feeding wires through, setting up screens, testing it all, and making adjustments. When James looked at his watch, it was nine in the evening. They had one hour to clean up before the club opened, and that meant James had to break the news to his brother—and there wasn't a more secure location in this building than in the crawl space of the ceiling.

"He's our guy," James whispered, taking the precaution even though he thought it unnecessary.

"Who?" Deacon said, looking up. His eyes widened as he realized whom James had meant. "Kyoji Tohmatsu? No way. The guy is a maniac."

"True," James said. "But he's smart, he's violent, and he doesn't hesitate. He has all the characteristics required for the job."

Deacon pinched the bridge of his nose. "Okay, so maybe he's well suited. But he has no reason to help us. He has protection—he has an army of loyal men backing him everywhere he goes. What can we offer him?"

James had given that a lot of thought today. "He has protection, and he has loyalty, but every single one of his men has something to gain from him. Money. Power. Respect. From the files we have on him, and from what I've seen in this club, he doesn't have anyone around him that's not a Tohmatsu. Yes, being in a gang brings support and loyalty, but that can also turn. We can offer him protection from an outside source—a source that has nothing to gain from the relationship—if he ever finds himself in a situation where he can't trust his own people. It wouldn't be the first time a gangster has found himself in that position. Look at the Russians."

Deacon nodded. The Russians were going through a bad spot— one not helped by the damage James and Deacon had done.

"Even if he does agree, you know there's one other problem, right?" Deacon asked, biting his lip.

James sighed. "Yeah. Haruki Tohmatsu."

It wasn't enough for Kyoji to agree; Haruki had to as well. James was much less confident about that negotiation.

"I think it's worth a shot at least," James said, and Deacon seemed to agree. Decisions were easily made when there were few options available.

5

KYOJI TOHMATSU

The air was hazy, laden with cigarette smoke, highlighted by the dimmed office lighting.

"What are your thoughts on them?" Kyoji asked.

Haruto drew a long drag, settling back against the couch cushion. He shrugged. "They know how to work. Other than that, it's a bit early to tell, don't you think?"

"I haven't had a chance to get a read on Deacon Thomas, but there's something different about James . . ."

"Other than the eyes?" Haruto joked.

James's blue eyes didn't match the black ones in his mug shot, and Kyoji had discussed that with Haruto. Kyoji concluded he was using contact lenses as a way to conceal his identity. He wondered what James's black eyes would look like in person—even in the photograph they looked like deep, bottomless wells. "And to think I thought I was the devil reincarnated."

Haruto sighed as he leaned forward to pour himself another glass.

"In all seriousness," Kyoji continued, "I get the sense he's hiding a lot."

"We're all hiding a lot."

There was no denying it, but James Thomas was different. He was a man who appeared so calm, yet Kyoji wondered if he might be the most dangerous man he'd ever come across. And that was a big statement to make.

"Time will tell," Kyoji said, hoping he wasn't going to find out the hard way. "They haven't stopped all day. I took a two-hour nap and still my eyes are raw—I don't think James Thomas has slept for days."

Kyoji butted his cigarette in the ashtray, already craving another. And the pussy that was waiting for him in bed. Once the Thomas brothers were done, he was going home to unwind for a few hours.

His cell phone lit up, and he was not surprised to see it was his uncle.

"It's all going well," Kyoji said, knowing the reason for his call. Haruki was nervous about the brothers installing the system, but ultimately Kyoji had made the decision. The fact that there were holes in his security made him anxious, but it wasn't the only reason he had agreed to let James do it. He also wanted his men to watch him, in the safety of their property. Kyoji couldn't shake the feeling that this man was important, but could he work out why he would be?

"Good. What have you learned?" Haruki asked.

"Not much," Kyoji admitted. "They work like soldiers—there's no doubting that. They're quiet, focused, efficient. I can't tell you anything else at this stage."

"Keep me informed. If I don't hear from you beforehand, I'll see you at dinner tomorrow evening."

"I'll call you if anything comes up," Kyoji said, the words barely out of his mouth before the call ended. He put his phone down on the table and heard a knock at his door.

"Come in," Kyoji called out.

The brothers entered side by side and Kyoji motioned for the couches. Haruto got up, coming to sit beside him.

"It's done," James said, handing over some rolled-up papers.

Kyoji laid them flat on the coffee table, noting that they were blueprints. He looked over them—a process made easier by the fact that all of the changes and improvements were noted on the papers. "I'm impressed." He truly was.

"Tell me," Kyoji said, looking at James, "why don't you do this for a living? It would keep you out of trouble."

"It doesn't pay as well. And it's not as much fun," James said, grinning.

Kyoji laughed. He didn't know why he liked the man, but he did. He'd liked him from their first meeting.

Kyoji turned his attention to Deacon. "You know, you two don't really look like brothers."

Deacon Thomas's lips curled. "You'll have to ask our mother about that."

Kyoji's eyes darted between them, not sure what to make of either of them, not really. And if they weren't causing trouble in Tokyo, he didn't really need to care—but he did. He was intrigued in a way that surprised him.

"Can we have a word?" James asked. "Privately."

Haruto looked to him and Kyoji nodded. When the door closed, he said, "This better be good."

James inhaled, his fingers forming a teepee. "A situation has arisen, evident by Tanaka's visit to Tokyo, and we need to know how far that extends."

James looked into his eyes, but Kyoji wasn't sure what he was looking for.

"I said nothing to Tanaka. I had no reason to," Kyoji said.

"That wasn't what I was getting at," James said with a subtle shake of his head. "We need someone to help us extract some information, seeing as we can't do it ourselves."

Kyoji's skin tingled. "And you think that person is me?"

How the fuck did they come up with that idea?

"Well, to clarify, we'll extract the information," Deacon said. "We just need you to extract the source."

Kyoji felt like he'd slipped into a dream—one he thought it would be best to wake up from very soon. "And by *extract the source*, what do you really mean?"

"We mean kidnap the source and bring her to us," James said.

Kyoji laughed, the sound slipping through his lips before he could stop it. His laugh disappeared when he realized he was the only one laughing. They were serious. "Why the fuck would I do that?" His eyebrows knitted together as his mind spun.

James answered. "Because we'll offer you something you don't have. Outside protection if a time comes that you can't trust your men. It'll be an open-ended favor—no expiration."

"You could disappear tomorrow and then so much for my favor," Kyoji said, pointing out the obvious.

"True. But when we give our word, we keep it. If we move, you'll be the only person we give our new number to. Your family, your clan, can make you vulnerable . . ." Deacon said. "Sometimes you need an extra set of eyes to watch over things."

They were serious. Deadly serious.

"I think you're both out of your minds," Kyoji said. "My answer is no. I can already tell you that. But I am intrigued to know . . . where exactly would this person be extracted from?"

"Russia. She's a CIA operative. She has the intel we need, but we can't go back there right now."

Deacon's jaw shifted, ever so subtly, and Kyoji wondered whether it was because he was displeased at what his brother had just revealed.

"I'll keep this between us," Kyoji said. "But the answer is still no. Not a fucking chance."

James held Kyoji's gaze, and Kyoji saw no defeat in his eyes. Instead he saw an unwavering, underlying sense of confidence. "Take some time to think about it—think about what we're offering you. What we've done with this," he said, motioning to the security system, "is like pre-school. We're making an offer to protect you, and potentially get you out of any shit you find yourself in, without question. Think about it. I'll come by again tomorrow."

"You'll be wasting your time," Kyoji said, lighting another cigarette.

"I'll take the chance," James said, before looking at his brother.

Deacon nodded then stood.

"Haruto will see you out," Kyoji said, knowing he'd be waiting outside.

The brothers left without another word, and Kyoji exhaled a long breath, keenly aware of the chill that had settled on his skin with their departure. Turning down their proposal made him uneasy— but he didn't understand why.

Kyoji slipped an arm around the pretty blonde's shoulders as she settled in for the night, curving her soft body against his.

He blew out a ring of smoke, staring blankly at the ceiling. He'd come three times, spanked her ass until it was blushing red, and still he couldn't shake the sense of foreboding that followed him like a shadow.

Kyoji thought over the proposal again. It was insanity. Only a madman would take that kind of risk for a favor he may never need to collect. Or be *able* to collect; the Thomas brothers disappearing, or getting killed, was a very real possibility.

And yet he couldn't stop thinking about it. What if there did come a time that he needed their services?

Kyoji wasn't sure what the Thomas brothers were capable of. How good were they, really? But his gut instincts combined with what he'd seen in the last few days told Kyoji they walked their talk. In fact, he'd even go as far to say they were modest in an attempt to hide how extensive their skill set truly was.

It pained Kyoji that he'd paid a security firm hundreds of thousands of dollars to assess and install new security systems in all of his clubs and homes, as well as Jayce's apartments, and James Thomas had walked in and performed a complete upgrade within twenty-four hours for free. It was without a doubt a blessing, but Kyoji just wished it'd happened a few months ago—before he'd blown the cash.

Kyoji sighed, throwing back the covers, burying the woman underneath.

"Hey!" she said, resurfacing.

Kyoji grinned. "I'll be back in a few minutes." He retrieved a robe from his closet and wandered into the kitchen, searching for a bottle of whiskey but only finding an empty one. "Damn it," Kyoji muttered. He owned a portfolio of clubs, and yet his own liquor supply was as dry as his mouth.

A rattle of keys sounded and Kyoji smiled, looking at the neon numbers on the microwave.

4:00 a.m.

Jayce was home from work.

"Hey, brother," Jayce said, depositing his briefcase on the dining table and taking a seat at the kitchen island. "What are you doing up?"

"Looking for some of this," he said with a frown, holding up the empty bottle.

Jayce's head tilted, a glint in his eyes.

"It's not funny," Kyoji said, turning the kettle on instead.

"You drank it, not me. Just call one of your boys to bring you another one," Jayce said.

Kyoji could, he'd certainly done it before, but he'd been looking for the whiskey as a distraction, and now he had a better one.

"I'll have a cup of tea with you instead," Kyoji said, putting a tea bag into each of the cups. "How was your day?"

Jayce sighed, rubbing his palms over his face. "It was fine, but I've been working on the restructuring plan. I'm convinced it's what we need to do, and the statistics support it, but people's lives are going to change. People will lose their jobs. I don't feel good about that."

"Of course you don't, but business is business," Kyoji said.

"I know," Jayce said without hesitation. He might have a conscience, but ultimately he was a Tohmatsu. They did what they needed to be done.

"Father isn't going to approve your restructuring plan if he doesn't believe in it. God knows he doesn't give us any favors," Kyoji said with a scoff. "He always did make us work twice as hard for everything."

Kyoji no longer worked for his father, though he had when the man had been co-leader of the Tohmatsu gang with his twin brother, Haruki. But Jayce did, and Jayce had been working his ass off since he was a child, their father carefully grooming him to be even more successful than he was. It was no accident that Jayce was vice president at his age, and it wasn't because he was the son of the CEO. Jayce had put in more hours in that company than most employees would in their lifetimes. Hence why he was getting home at four on a Sunday morning—and that wasn't abnormal.

Kyoji turned the kettle off just before boiling point and poured the tea, taking one over to Jayce.

"Why are you home?" Jayce asked, checking his watch as if he'd misread the time.

"I was at the club all day. I had a new security system fitted," Kyoji said.

Jayce's eyes widened. "Another one? Why, what's going on?"

Kyoji shook his head. Even if something were going on, he wouldn't tell Jayce—he wouldn't want to worry him. "Nothing, but I met someone recently who's an expert in this, better even than the company I used previously. I thought it couldn't hurt." Kyoji took a sip of his tea while looking longingly at the whiskey bottle. "I'm going to get the guy to fit out this apartment too."

Jayce shrugged nonchalantly. "If you want."

Jayce never worried about security—he didn't need to, because Kyoji always made sure he was taken care of. Always. He swore he'd loved that kid since his step-mother had first introduced them.

Wanting to take care of Jayce—to protect him—was one of the reasons Kyoji lived with Jayce, in Jayce's apartment. Kyoji had plenty of apartments of his own but living with Jayce gave him a chance to keep an eye on him, given their schedules were hardly compatible. It was random talks like this that kept them connected.

"Kyoji?"

Jayce didn't even bat an eyelid at the sound of the woman's voice.

"Yeah, I'll be there soon," Kyoji said, rolling his eyes.

Jayce smirked and then whispered, "You're an asshole."

"She's demanding. I thought that was attractive a few hours ago," Kyoji said with a hushed voice.

Jayce chuckled under his breath. "I'm glad I missed all of that." He drank the last of his tea and pushed the cup away.

"Okay, I'm going to get a few hours of sleep before heading back to the office," Jayce said, his eyes cast down on his phone. The kid never stopped working.

"Good night, little brother," Kyoji said, putting their teacups in the dishwasher.

Instead of going back to bed, though, he walked over to the windows, looking down on the matrix of colored squares and blinking lights floating in the dark abyss.

That sense of apprehension seized him once more. Truthfully, he wasn't worried about protecting himself, but there was always one thought that plagued him: Would Jayce be okay if Kyoji wasn't there to protect him? Jayce had security through the Tohmatsu family, and their father would ensure he was protected, but would it be good enough? What if Kyoji was turning down the opportunity to guarantee Jayce had another layer of security if something happened to him? God only knew when his own expiration date was, considering the life he led.

But was the mission the Thomas brothers offered a death mission in itself?

And would it bring trouble back to Tokyo?

6

JAMES THOMAS

James sipped on his cup of coffee, letting the mug warm his hands. He didn't need to look at the time again—he'd been impatiently watching the clock for hours. Given the situation and their need to act quickly, James couldn't think of anyone better suited for their mission than Kyoji, but the man also had a lot of reasons to turn it down. And given his refusal yesterday, James wasn't particularly hopeful, but there was a spark of optimism in his chest, flickering softly.

"These are the monthly reports," Nicole said, placing a folder in front of him.

"Thanks." James would look over them in due time, but right now his mind was focused on staying alive and staying in Tokyo.

"Do you really think Kyoji's going to change his mind?" she asked, resting her fingertips on the table.

James shrugged. "Unlikely, but it's worth visiting him again." He slid out of his chair. "On that note, I'm going to get going. Thanks for these." He nodded at the papers. "I'll look over them tonight."

"James . . ." Nicole's voice stopped him. "What do you really think we should do? Do you think we should leave Tokyo?" she asked, seeming to hold her breath.

Yes. "I think we need more information before we make that decision. Even if we decided to leave tomorrow, without knowing where they're looking for us, we could go somewhere else and put ourselves in more danger," he said, giving her a half truth.

She chewed on her bottom lip, but James thought she bought his answer. Eventually, she nodded. "If I don't see you before I go to the safe house, be careful. And please take care of him," she said, holding his gaze. She gave a small smile. "I think you're the brother he always wanted. Life has a funny way of working out, doesn't it?"

James paused—he'd never considered if Deacon felt that way. "It sure does," he said. "I'll take care of him, Nicole. I'll do everything I can to keep him safe. To keep you both safe."

"I know," she said with a quiet yet strong voice. James didn't believe she doubted him. And nor should she. He didn't approve of their relationship, but that didn't mean he wouldn't do everything he could to take care of both of them.

He gave her a smile he hoped relieved some of her worry and picked up his keys. "Make sure your bags are packed for the safe house. We need to be ready to leave at a moment's notice."

"I'll do it now. Thank you, James," she said, searching his eyes one last time before moving toward the bedroom she shared with Deacon.

James picked up his car keys and took the elevator to the basement. The drive across town to Kyoji's club took longer than anticipated, but he still arrived early—he'd left the house earlier than intended.

"Kyoji's expecting me," James said to the bouncer, who was as unfriendly today as every other day James had seen him.

A small nod was the only indication the man had heard him. The bouncer unlocked the door and James entered to find one of Kyoji's men waiting.

"This way," the young man said.

James guessed he was sixteen at most, but it was hard to tell.

Kyoji sat at his desk, and it was one of the few times James had seen him without a cigarette between his fingers.

"Aren't you the optimist?" Kyoji asked.

"I get that the odds aren't in my favor. Then again, I've made a life of defying the odds, so I've got no reason to stop now," James said, taking a seat opposite the gangster.

"I believe you"—Kyoji folded his hands on the table—"and that's the problem. I'm not sure why I should. Or why I should believe anything you tell me. But I do. Usually I'm a much colder, less welcoming guy."

"I wouldn't exactly call you warm," James said with a wink.

Kyoji wiggled his eyebrows. "Tell me more about this proposition of yours. Tell me exactly what you would want me to do."

James took a deep breath. It was a risk to detail the plan to Kyoji —James didn't know all of his friends—but he also didn't expect the man to agree to help them without the details. The fact that Kyoji had even asked the question gave James hope.

"Deacon and I will go with you, but we can't show our faces in Russia. We can't even be seen on the streets," James said. "There's too much heat from some recent activity there."

Kyoji nodded, and then James detailed their plan.

Kyoji's face remained impassive, but James had no doubt his mind was spinning with questions.

"So, if things go wrong, who the fuck is going to back me up?" Kyoji asked with hard eyes.

"We'll never be far away. But, if things really go pear-shaped, then we'll have no choice but to retrieve you—even if that means showing our faces."

"And your chance of getting me before they kill me?"

"High, actually," James said with an inappropriate smile. "If you mention the name Liam Smith, and tell them I'm coming for you, they'll keep you alive. I can't promise you they'll play nice in the meantime, though."

"Fucking hell," Kyoji swore under his breath. "The offer you propose isn't good enough—I would want more in return."

James's heart skipped a beat. The crazy bastard was going to do it. "Name your price."

"If the time comes when I need protection, I want it for any family member. If I'm dead before the favor is cashed in, it gets transferred to Jayce."

James nodded. "We'll protect your immediate family, but not Haruki's—that's not something I can commit to. Transferring it to Jayce is not a problem."

"I also want every single premise I own, and Jayce's, to have full security fit-outs done . . . complimentary, of course."

"Agreed, but that has to wait until after you've done your part. I need this information—I needed it yesterday," James said, holding Kyoji's gaze.

"One more thing," Kyoji said, a challenge in his eyes. "When you extract the information, I'll be present. I promise you I won't speak a word of what is overheard, but if you're getting me involved in this, I want to know who you are and what you've done. And that's not negotiable."

If they'd had another option, James would've told Kyoji no. But they didn't. "Agreed." James hoped he wasn't going to regret that part of the deal.

Kyoji leaned back in his chair, folding his arms over his chest. "When do you want to leave?"

"Tonight," James said without hesitation. They'd wasted enough time already.

"No, not a chance," Kyoji said, shaking his head. "It's Jayce's birthday tomorrow. We'll leave the day after."

James took a calming breath. "Kyoji, this is urgent. We don't have the luxury of time. If they send more men, I could be dead tomorrow."

Kyoji shrugged. "I've never missed one of his birthdays, and I'm not about to start now."

It was just a birthday. James didn't even know when his own birthday was.

"Kyoji—" James started before he was cut off.

"Take it or leave it, Thomas. I'll go with you on Tuesday, or you can find someone else to do the job if you want it done before then," he said with a sly grin.

James reeled in his frustration. "You've got a deal. I'll book the flights. Be ready to leave at one minute past midnight."

"Book the flights?" Kyoji asked with a scoff. "I don't fly commercial. Send me the details, and I'll organize the jet." Kyoji paused, a wicked grin lighting up his face. "Maybe I'll bring some in-house entertainment. A good fuck might be just what you need."

Kyoji wasn't wrong. James stood, chuckling. "Organize it for the way home when we've got something to celebrate. Until then, be in battle mode. I'll be in touch."

James cracked his knuckles one after the other as he sat in the car, idling on the tarmac. They were supposed to have departed five minutes ago and Kyoji was nowhere to be found. Nor was he answering his cell phone.

"This is so bad," Deacon said with a hushed voice, like he didn't want to speak the words—the truth.

"I know," James murmured. They'd wasted time waiting for Kyoji, and James couldn't believe he wasn't here.

Waiting for thirty hours for someone might not seem like a big deal, but when you had a guy like Tanaka hunting you, and getting as close as he did, every minute counted.

James released a strained sigh. He didn't know what to do. Did they leave now and go to the airport on their own? But that meant that they, or at least James, would have to go into Russia. Everyone was looking for them—mafia, Interpol, police. His chances of making it out were as good as Deacon becoming the next president.

James almost jumped when his cell phone vibrated in his hands: *Kyoji Tohmatsu.*

Kyoji started speaking before James said a word. "I'm on my way. Something came up last minute and I couldn't leave until it was dealt with. I'll be there in thirty minutes."

James wasn't happy about the delay, but at least Kyoji was coming. "We'll see you soon," he said and ended the call.

Deacon looked at him expectantly.

"He's on his way. Something came up," James said, pressing his lips together, noting Deacon's long inhale and tight shoulders. James didn't think it was entirely the result of frustration, but also nerves. Deacon was leaving behind the woman he loved and was hoping he was going to return to her—with good news.

James's eyelids were heavy, but he fought the urge to close them. Until they were up in the air, he needed to stay alert. His eyes swept over their surroundings once again as they sat behind the protection of their armored vehicle. It was an expensive car, one they'd stretched their first paycheck from Saito to buy, but it was worth every dollar. And it made Deacon happy—it was fast.

Thirty-two minutes later a black sedan came to a halt on the tarmac beside them and Kyoji jumped out, waving. He took the stairs two at a time, straight onto the jet. The brothers looked at each other with raised eyebrows and got out of the car, following him. Kyoji was in the cockpit with the pilot when they boarded.

"Take a seat anywhere," Kyoji called, looking over his shoulder for a moment before returning his attention to the pilot.

James took a seat on the lounge chair, and Deacon sat opposite him. Kyoji joined them a moment later.

"Fucking hell, what a night," Kyoji said, throwing his bag down beside James. "Sorry to give you a scare, boys."

James refrained from saying what he really wanted to. "No problem. You're here now."

Kyoji grinned. "So, what are we going to talk about for the next thirteen hours?"

7

KYOJI TOHMATSU

Kyoji's eyes darted between the two brothers, watching their reactions. It was hard to read them, Deacon Thomas less so than James. He either couldn't completely conceal his feelings or, more likely, he didn't want to. And Kyoji didn't entirely blame him—if the situation had been reversed he'd be pissed, too.

"I'd like to get some sleep, actually," James said, rubbing his eyes. "When we land, there won't be much time for sleeping. I suggest you take advantage of this time, too."

Kyoji grinned. "Yes, sir."

Kyoji was tired, definitely, but after the negotiation he'd just had with his uncle he doubted he'd be able to sleep.

Haruki had had a last minute change of heart, pulling back his approval for Kyoji to go with the brothers. It'd taken Kyoji two hours to convince him otherwise, and he couldn't help but feel like he'd taken the tension with him—it seemed to cling to his skin.

What if he was making a big mistake?

What if this led the CIA back to Tokyo? That could have huge implications for the Tohmatsu family.

But as he looked at James again, he got that same sense of conviction. From every angle it looked like a bad decision, but his gut told him otherwise.

Kyoji didn't blame his uncle for thinking the way he had, and he thought it was a small miracle that he was on this plane right now.

This could be a turning point in his life. He hoped that what was around the corner was worth it.

∼

Kyoji's eyes flung open as the jet shuddered. He released the breath he'd been holding when he realized it was just a patch of turbulence, and that they weren't falling from the sky.

He cast his eyes over the cabin. Both brothers were reclined in chairs, blankets pulled up to their chins. He'd thought they were sleeping, but then James opened his eyes, looking straight at Kyoji.

"Can't sleep?" James asked.

"It's a bit fucking bumpy, don't you think?" Kyoji asked as the plane shook again, its windows rattling, sending his stomach lurching.

James gave a thin smile. "There are worse ways to die."

Kyoji scoffed. There were more painful ways to die, sure, but he wasn't certain if there was a more terrifying way.

"How does he sleep through this?" Kyoji tilted his head toward Deacon.

James shrugged. "He's done a lot of flying in his time."

Kyoji mulled on that, knowing James wasn't going to give him anything more.

Why had Deacon done a lot of flying? Kyoji had assumed he'd also been CIA, but perhaps that was an incorrect assumption. There were so many questions Kyoji wanted to ask. He hoped this trip would answer some of them, indirectly or otherwise.

Another violent tremor caused Kyoji to clutch his armrests as everything around him to shake. Deacon's eyes opened, paused, as if perhaps assessing the situation, and then closed again.

Unbelievable, Kyoji thought, and then looked at his watch.

Five more hours.

God help us.

After a long flight, they'd safely descended into the lush, dense green fields of Polotsk—a view that was worthy of a postcard—however, James had apparently found the oldest apartment in Belarus's oldest town.

"Well, this is a fucking dive," Kyoji said, looking over their temporary digs, his nose scrunching as he breathed in the stale air.

"It serves its purpose," James said, depositing his overnight bag on the floral couch that Kyoji refused to even sit on.

"And that purpose would be?" Kyoji couldn't imagine that James wanted to pick up a disease, but there were surely plenty lurking on that couch.

"Privacy. If trouble follows us back here, we can make noise and the cops won't come—at least not immediately."

They'd landed an hour ago, picked up their rental car, and driven to the apartment.

"I can't fathom why the cops would've deserted this hell," Kyoji mumbled under his breath. He placed his bag on the wooden kitchen table, concluding it was less of a breeding ground than the couch.

Kyoji watched as James retrieved items from his bag—notably, all weapons—and started strapping them onto his body.

"Did you walk into my club like that the first time you snuck in?" Kyoji asked, already knowing the answer.

"You bet I did." James flashed him a half-cocked grin. "Now, I'm going out to get a few things. I'll bring dinner back with me, and then we'll be leaving in a few hours."

"Do you need some help?" Kyoji asked, interested to see James Thomas at work on the streets.

James shook his head. "I'll be faster on my own," he said as he slid his pistol into the back of his jeans and left without another word.

~

When James returned, he came with a bag of goodies. He first handed Kyoji a cell phone.

"It's a burner phone. You can take your cell phone with you as well, but all communication between the three of us is done via the burner phone. The numbers are already programmed in."

James held up a plastic sports watch.

"This device has a built in distress signal and your coordinates. Just press this button," James said, showing Kyoji. "This is for the worst-case scenario—and by that I mean the Russians are about to take you. Don't press it before then."

Kyoji took off his designer watch, strapping on the new one. "Can't they make one that looks better than this junk? I look cheap."

Deacon snorted, and James even smiled. "They do, but unfortunately we don't have access to that level of sophistication right now. Go join the CIA if you want cool-looking stuff."

Kyoji grinned. "You must miss the toys. What cool gadgets did you have?"

James ignored the question—he was clearly in battle mode. "Take off your shoes," he said.

Kyoji's sighed, not used to being given orders, but did as instructed. He watched keenly as James inserted several blades into the inner fabric of his trainers.

"If you find yourself on your knees with your hands tied behind your back, your best weapon will be one of these blades. They're different sizes," he said, pointing to the first blade. "This one will cut rope." He pointed to the next blade. "This one you can use to try and pick the lock—if they handcuff you. There's one of each in each shoe. They're damn sharp, so be careful you don't cut yourself in the process."

Next he threw Kyoji a ziplock bag stuffed full of sachets.

"Salt, blood-clotting agents, anti-bacterial wipes, bandages. I assume you know how to use this stuff?" James asked.

Unfortunately, Kyoji did, and he had the scars to prove it.

"I'll have a bigger medical kit for any surgery that's required," James said, his head down, searching through his bag.

"Surgery?" Kyoji asked. "Fuck, Thomas. You're really filling me with confidence."

"It's better to be overprepared," Deacon said, casually.

Kyoji got the feeling this was an everyday preparation for them. "By the way, which one of you is the surgeon?"

James gave him that same cocked grin. "Let's hope we don't have to find out."

Kyoji swore under his breath as he packed his mini medical kit in his bag.

"Lastly," James said, passing over a small black box.

Kyoji opened it carefully.

"Earpieces, listening devices, cameras," James said. "We'll show you how to use them on the drive. Let's eat, then we can get going."

Kyoji zipped the black box in his bag and sat down at the table for dinner.

He hoped it wasn't his last meal.

The road was thin and windy and Kyoji had to concentrate just to keep the van on the road. The car was quiet and had been for the entire drive.

"You're sure your papers are going to clear, right?" Kyoji asked, his eyes flickering down to the faux passport and visa that sat in his lap.

"They'll pass. We're using this route because the security at the border is minimal," James said, sitting in the back seat.

He was wearing his contacts—Kyoji had never seen him without them. He also had a cap on, and a jacket with a hood. He looked remarkably different than the man in his mug shot and every bit like the man pictured in the passport he held in his hands.

Deacon Thomas was in the passenger seat and Kyoji assumed there was a strategy to their seating, but they hadn't shared it with him.

Kyoji slowed as he saw the security crossing ahead. It was a strange predicament for him to be in, and one he wasn't used to—worrying about the law. In Tokyo, he had the power to do what he wanted with very little repercussions. Today, he felt like a fish swimming in the ocean hoping a shark wasn't lurking close by.

Kyoji brought the car to a stop as indicated by the man at the crossing and his heart thumped in his ears. He took a deep, calming breath as he lowered the window and handed over their papers.

The man looked at each paper in turn, comparing the photographs of the men to the passports. He paused on Deacon's, and then said, "Pozhaluysta, podozhdite."

Kyoji watched the man walk away, his hands sweating on the steering wheel.

"What did he say?" Kyoji whispered.

"Please wait," James answered quietly.

"Wait for what?" Kyoji asked, tentatively.

"I'm not sure," James said.

Kyoji's eyes met his in the rearview mirror. James gave a reassuring nod.

The car continued to hum, its emissions swirling behind them like white smoke. Minutes passed before the man returned.

"Preuspevat," the man said, handing back the documents.

Kyoji had no idea what the man said—but Deacon whispered, "Drive."

He slowly pressed his foot down on the accelerator, careful not to speed off despite his racing pulse, and drove into Russia.

Deacon blew out a sigh that sounded like a whistle, and Kyoji was glad that he hadn't been the only one feeling the heat.

"What was he doing?" Kyoji asked.

Deacon shook his head, twisting to look over his shoulder.

"I don't know either," James said. "But it doesn't matter. Keep driving for another twenty minutes, then we'll pull over and Deacon will drive. You did well," James said like a teacher might say to a student.

"Why does Deacon get to drive?" Kyoji asked.

"Because he's the best driver you'll ever meet," James said, and Deacon flashed the kind of smile worn by Hollywood movie stars.

8

JAMES THOMAS

James relaxed his grip, taking his finger off the trigger. That had been close—too close. They'd made it through the border crossing, but James didn't know if that was because they'd gone undetected or if border security had let them pass through only to put out an alert of their arrival. Whatever happened at the border crossing, though, James had no intention of telling Kyoji just how worried he was.

"Pull over here," James said, eager to get Deacon behind the wheel.

They swapped over and immediately James felt a sense of calm wash over him. He felt more in control for anything that might come up.

But nothing did.

They drove for over seven hours before they reached Moscow.

They checked into a rundown motel, and James didn't miss the pouty look on Kyoji's face. The guy was too used to luxury accommodations.

"Seriously, do we have to stay here?" Kyoji asked, lighting up a cigarette.

"Yes, we do," Deacon said, looking somewhat amused. "If you think this is bad, you should see some of the places we've stayed in."

Kyoji scrunched up his face. "How the two of you don't have herpes I will never understand . . . or maybe you do?"

Deacon snorted. "Prince Kyoji, you live a hard life."

James grinned at the banter between them, but his mind was already strategizing. He looked out of the window and up at the black clouds, which were parting only to reveal pockets of vibrant indigo. Darkness was almost upon them, and tonight they would hide in its shadows.

"Any questions?" James asked, and Kyoji shook his head. Kyoji was wired up, loaded with weapons, and that was all James could do for him. He was on his own now, in a city he didn't know, with men he should definitely fear.

James had used the hours in the car to load a series of files onto Kyoji's phone. Mostly the files were photographs—mug-shot style—of faces he should be aware of. Faces he should run from should he see them.

James handed Kyoji one last item. "Keep this in your pocket."

Kyoji pressed his lips together, holding the syringe between his fingers. "How do you know this is going to sedate her and not kill her? I don't need to be you to know that murdering a CIA agent is going to get me in a heap of shit."

"It's enough to sedate her for a few hours—long enough for us to get her to a secure location."

"Great," Kyoji muttered, still looking at the syringe.

They loaded into the car and Deacon drove. If all went to plan, the Thomas brothers would never be leaving the car tonight—until they got to the next piece-of-junk hotel. Even James didn't like their accommodation, but he wasn't going to admit it to Kyoji.

Deacon pulled the car to a stop forty minutes later. They all looked among one another.

"Good luck," James said. Kyoji was going to need it.

Kyoji nodded and got out of the car, slipping into the shadows of the building.

"Do you really think he can do this?" Deacon whispered.

"I don't know, but I do think he's our best chance," James said, massaging his temples.

It took Kyoji fifteen minutes to reach Angela's apartment on foot, and James fought to control his mind the entire time. It reeled with possible scenarios, very few of them good.

"Checking in. Lights are on, curtains are drawn," Kyoji's voice came through James's earpiece.

"Copy. Find somewhere you can wait and watch," James said.

They didn't know Angela's schedule, and they had no source of intel to obtain it, so they were doing it the old-fashioned way—on foot. Kyoji could be sitting in the cold air, freezing his ass off for hours. And if so, James knew they were going to hear about it.

"Copy. Location secure. This piece of pussy better be worth it," Kyoji said, and the brothers looked at each other. Deacon looked like he might giggle.

"Focus, Kyoji," James said, hiding the amusement from his voice.

"Yeah, yeah," Kyoji mumbled.

A minute later: *"Do you know how fucking cold it is?"* Kyoji asked.

"I don't know. It's warm where we are," Deacon said with sparkling eyes.

James shook his head but grinned when Kyoji answered. *"Fuck you both. My dick is going to freeze off. What kind of life am I going to have—?"*

"Kyoji?" James asked, his pulse spiking.

"She just walked out the front door. The lights are still on," he said, his voice now barely audible.

"Follow her. Keep a safe distance," James said. Not being beside Kyoji, in the heart of the action, was about as painful as pulling out a tooth without anesthetic. James's body was itching to get out of the car and join in, but he knew he couldn't; if anyone saw through his disguise and recognized him for who he was, it was very unlikely they would get out of Russia alive.

James looked at the screen of the device tracking Kyoji, following him on the map.

"She's got a nice ass," Kyoji said under his breath.

James ignored him, wondering where Angela was going at this time of night—alone.

"What is she wearing?" James asked.

"Tight black jeans," Kyoji said, and James rolled his eyes.

"What *else* is she wearing?"

"Why?"

"When I ask you a question, answer it," James said, his sense of humor long gone. "You might not get a second chance," James warned.

"She's wearing black jeans, ankle boots—no heel—and a black puffy jacket with a fur-lined hood."

"Where are her hands?" James asked.

"In her jacket pocket. I don't know if she's got gloves on."

"She won't," James said. Gloves made it very difficult to wield weapons, and that was why Angela's hands were in her jacket instead, keeping them warm and nimble.

"She'll be holding a weapon in her hands," James said.

Kyoji muttered, *"Crazy bitch."*

"Drop back—you're too close," James said, now able to see Angela in the footage from Kyoji's camera. The last thing they needed was to tip her off. Kyoji was going to get only one chance to do this, and there was no way in hell he would succeed if she were suspicious she were being followed.

"I'll bet she's a crazy bitch in bed, too," Kyoji whispered.

James knew the answer to that, but it wasn't something he was sharing with Kyoji.

"She's slowing down," Kyoji whispered. *"419—that's the building she just entered."*

Deacon quickly typed it into their laptop. "It looks like it's a residential apartment block."

That could be very bad news for Kyoji—if Angela was going for a sleepover, he was going to have a long night out in the cold.

"Are you secure?" James asked.

"Copy. You know, this is really not as much fun as I thought it'd be," he said.

It never was. The life of agents, of spies, of espionage—most of it was spent watching and waiting. James wondered how many hours of his life he'd spent doing exactly that. *A lot*, he concluded, not able to come up with a number. And if all went as planned, there'd be even more hours of it in his future.

"Kyoji, what's across the street, two doors down?" Deacon asked, his fingers typing on the keyboard.

"A café or diner of some kind," Kyoji said vaguely.

"Will you have a clear view of the apartment entrance from there?" Deacon asked.

"Yes, if I sit at one of the window tables."

Deacon looked to James and he nodded. "Go inside and get a cup of coffee—we'll tell you what to say. You could be waiting a while, and it will keep you warm. But keep your eyes on that apartment —discreetly."

"Got it," Kyoji said with renewed vigor.

Deacon pressed his ear, deactivating his earpiece. "Who do you think she's visiting?"

James pressed his lips together. "Likely a contact or colleague. People like Angela—like me—don't keep friends. They ask too many questions."

Deacon nodded. "Hopefully she doesn't stay long."

"I'm approaching the counter," Kyoji said.

James gave him a Russian translation, which Kyoji fumbled through, but it didn't matter; he hardly looked like a local. But at least his gloves concealed the tattoos across Kyoji's knuckles—tattoos that indicated he was the vice president of the Tohmatsu clan. In Russia, that wasn't a message they wanted to promote.

A few minutes later Kyoji spoke again, *"Seated."*

James looked at his watch, noting the time.

"A light just activated on the fourth floor, second window from the

right," Kyoji said, his voice low, hushed. *"Shit, I can see her . . . or, I could see her . . . she just closed the curtains."*

"Okay. Hold and wait," James instructed.

"Fuck," Kyoji swore. *"She's moving. She's crossing the street . . . she's coming in here."*

"Pretend you're reading something on your cell phone," James said calmly, but the anticipation had gripped him, adrenaline seeping into his veins.

Come on, Kyoji. Pull this off.

"What's she doing?" Deacon asked.

"I don't know. You really should've taught me to speak Russian," Kyoji whispered. *"She's got a drink of some sort. Takeout."*

"Get up and leave now," James said. "Go to the south corner and wait. Listen for her footsteps. Have the syringe ready in your hand."

James doubted this was Kyoji's first time capturing someone, but it was almost certainly his first encounter with a CIA agent—a skilled one, at that.

"Copy."

James reminded himself to breathe.

"In position," Kyoji said.

"Put your mask on," James instructed. Kyoji being recognized could definitely lead trouble back to Tokyo.

"Copy. She's coming."

James closed his eyes and said a silent prayer.

9

KYOJI TOHMATSU

The echo of her footsteps bounced off the concrete walkway.

Don't fuck this up, Kyoji.

His earpiece was silent. He was on his own. On a random street in Moscow, about to kidnap a CIA agent. He'd done some crazy shit, but this was at the top of the list.

There's no turning back from this, Kyoji thought to himself, but his decision was already made. He'd come this far—he wasn't going to back down now. Given her winter attire, he had no other option but to jab her where her skin was exposed. It was risky, but everything about this job was risky.

He inhaled until his chest burned, and then slowly exhaled, listening to her steps.

Three, two, one . . .

The woman stepped out in front of him and Kyoji lunged.

She saw him in her peripheral vision, her eyes doubling in size.

Kyoji slammed the syringe into her neck, fumbling the plunger as her scream pierced his ears, and her arm swung up.

Her fist connected with his cheek, and he lost his grip on the syringe.

She raised her weapon but Kyoji knocked it from her arms, sending it flying across the street.

She reached for the syringe, yanking it out. Kyoji reached for it at the same time, noting that the plunger was fully in.

"What have you done?" she asked, backing away.

Kyoji grabbed her jacket, pulling her back into the alley. But as he did he looked up to see a figure streaking past the window. Someone had been watching her. And now they were coming.

Angela swayed and Kyoji grabbed her, taking her weight as her knees began to buckle.

"Boys, I've got company," Kyoji hissed. "Get me the fuck out of here!"

Angela collapsed in his arms, almost taking him down with her.

"Two seconds," James voice came through the earpiece, and Kyoji heard a sickening thud before a car came to a screeching stop on the curb.

"Come on!" James yelled and Kyoji hauled Angela's limp body to the back seat. James helped load their captive. Kyoji jumped in last and Deacon had his foot down before the door was closed.

Kyoji swore, looking at the body in the middle of the street behind them. "Fuck me. Did you run over him?"

"He bounced off the bonnet," James said without a hint of emotion in his voice.

"And good job," James said just as the glass behind them shattered.

"Hold on, boys!" Deacon shouted as he swung the car around a corner.

Kyoji stole a peek through what had been the rear window.

A man on a motorcycle.

James turned around, kneeling on the back seat and started firing. Kyoji didn't wait to be told what to do—he copied James and soon a shot hit and the man fell from the bike, sliding across the street.

"Go! Go! Go!" James yelled, and Kyoji gripped the armrest for stability as the car lurched over a sidewalk and then back onto the road.

Kyoji's heart drummed in his ears, his legs weightless. He looked out of the rear of the car again, but there was no one behind them.

"Are you okay?" James asked.

"I'm fine. She pulled her pistol, but I managed to deflect it," Kyoji said, his stomach souring at his next thought. "Fuck, it's in the alley. I forgot to pick it up."

James shook his head. "It's okay. We've caused enough of a scene that the CIA will know she was targeted anyway. Finding her weapon won't make a difference."

James put his fingers to Angela's slouched neck—the only thing holding her up was Kyoji's shoulder. James seemed to be checking her pulse, but when he lifted his fingers and turned his attention to the street behind them Kyoji assumed the woman wasn't dying.

"We need to change cars," James said. "The sooner the better."

Deacon gave a nod of his head. "Agreed. I'll find something suitable."

A few minutes later Deacon pulled the car over. He got out, and Kyoji's eyes followed him as he broke into their new car and hotwired it.

"He's got an interesting set of skills," Kyoji said.

James grinned. "He's not just a pretty face," he said, and Kyoji chortled.

Deacon leaned in. "Let's go, boys."

Kyoji and James transferred Angela into their new car while Deacon did a full check, making sure they hadn't left anything behind.

The journey to the hotel they were using for the interrogation was quiet, but Kyoji didn't let himself relax. Not yet. Until he was back on the jet he wouldn't let his guard down.

At the hotel, James disappeared into the lobby and came back a few minutes later, a key dangling from his hand.

"Drive around the back," he said to Deacon, pointing.

It was another dive. *At least I don't have to sleep in this one*, Kyoji thought.

They parked at the rear of the building, directly in front of door fifty-three. James unlocked it, did a check, and then motioned them in. Kyoji and Deacon hung Angela's arms over their shoulders, carrying her weight. For anyone passing by, they likely looked like two guys helping a friend home—one that'd had more vodka than she should've.

They put Angela on a dining chair, and James bound her arms and legs. He rummaged through his medical kit, pulling out two clear vials. He drew a dose, injected it into a vein in her arm, and then repeated it with a dose from the second vial.

James looked to Kyoji. "What you hear next does not leave this room."

Now things were going to get very interesting.

Kyoji smiled wide.

Very interesting indeed.

10

JAMES THOMAS

Angela's eyelids fluttered and her body trembled as it broke through the holds of the sedation—helped by a dose of reversal. Slowly, her eyes opened.

"You're safe," James said, wondering if her brain would recognize his voice through the haze.

It took a moment, and her mind seemed to clear. Her pupils dilated and she fought against the restraints.

"Liam!" she growled through gritted teeth.

"Sorry," he said. "I didn't have a lot of options. I gave you some meds to reduce any nausea."

"And you want a thank you for that?" Her voice was cold, her words clipped.

James didn't blame her—he would've had the same reaction, or worse. Likely much worse.

"I'm sorry, Ange, but I need your help. I wouldn't have done this otherwise," James said.

"Help? You're a wanted man. You shouldn't even be here. You can't move around the streets of Russia and expect to leave alive," she said, her voice sounding more alert, and less pissed off, and that gave James hope. Hope that she might help him.

"I'm not walking around the streets. I have someone else to do that. And I plan on leaving as soon as I have the information I need. Information you have access to," James said, leaning forward.

"Undo my arms," Angela said.

James shook his head. "Talk first."

Her teeth sawed together.

"Let's not do this the hard way," he said, keeping his frustration out of his voice. She was wasting time, and he wanted to leave before the sun rose. The more distance they could get between themselves and Moscow, the safer they would be.

"You're a cold son of a bitch," she said.

James ignored the jab.

She resisted for another few seconds, and then she sighed angrily. "What do you want to know?"

"I want to know who the CIA has assigned to look for me. And I want to know what leads they have, and where they're looking. All information your access will give you."

"It's not who, singular—it's who, plural. They've assigned a task force, Liam. A thirty-person unit dedicated to one mission and one mission only: Capture Liam Smith. Dead or alive."

A team. It was worse than he thought. James narrowed his eyes slightly.

"I need you to log in. I need you to see where they're looking."

She hesitated, and his heart skipped a beat. What was she hiding?

"Ange," James warned.

"I don't need to log in," she said, meeting his eyes.

It took a moment to register.

"You're one of the thirty, aren't you?" James said, letting the disgust drip through his words. He'd never had friends, but he thought he'd had a few allies. He'd thought she was one of them.

"I'm a non-participating member, yes," she said. "Don't look at me like that. You know damn well I couldn't refuse that mission or they'd start looking into me, too. Our relationship—of sorts—complicated things. You made a fucking mess, Liam. You can't assassinate eighty percent of the Russian mafia and the head of the CIA and not expect repercussions."

In his peripheral vision he saw Kyoji's eyes widen. The man knew far too much already.

"Define *non-participating member*," James said, returning his attention the conversation. His gaze stony.

"I attend the meetings. I pretend I'm doing something useful. I file the same report week after week: nil associations or leads on target." She looked him straight in the eyes. "The same report I'll file next week."

James cocked an eyebrow. Did he believe her? The only reason she would be if she feared him more than she feared the CIA—which was a possibility.

"Who were you visiting tonight? He ran in front of the car, and I didn't stop to check if he was alive. Questions will be asked," James said. This kidnapping situation just got a hell of a lot more complicated.

"Well done, you potentially killed our only link to an Arabian gang that's trying to infiltrate Russia. The case has nothing to do with you."

If she was telling the truth, that little non-accident could've been the smartest move they made. It would look like a gang hit, so that no one would have cause to suspect Liam Smith's involvement.

If she was telling the truth.

"I want you to load the last report on me. I want to see it," James said. "I'm going to undo your hands—keep your eyes on me. Turn your head and it will be the last thing you'll ever see." He would do her no favors because he'd shared her bed.

"Unfortunately, I believe you," she said. "I can tell you what the last report said. They don't have any leads on you—that's the problem. That's why they've increased the size of the task force."

Why was Tanaka looking for him in Tokyo, then? It didn't make sense.

James nodded to Deacon, and he cut Ange's hands free. "I want to read the report. Load it," James said.

The reasons he wanted to see it with his own eyes were twofold: he wanted to make sure she wasn't lying, of course, but he also wanted to see if Tanaka was listed as a member of the task force. If he wasn't, who had sent him?

James handed Ange a laptop. There was one advantage to her being on the taskforce—accessing his files wouldn't raise any questions.

She typed a series of codes—passwords—and then turned the laptop to him.

With Deacon and Kyoji to watch his back, James's eyes dropped to the screen. This particular report was thirty pages long—he'd need to download it and read it in full—but for now he scanned it, looking for one code name. He didn't see it.

She wasn't lying about the leads, though. They had nothing on Tokyo. Not a single lead.

But someone did. Someone had sent Tanaka.

He weighed his next words carefully.

"This report doesn't mention Paris," James said, using Tanaka's last known location.

Her eyebrows threaded together. "Why would it?"

"Because I ran into an old friend of ours, one who was asking for me."

She seemed genuinely confused, but she was a trained spy.

"Timothy Tanaka."

At the mention of his name her lips pursed.

"Then you're facing a very different problem," she said. "Tanaka went rogue five months ago."

The pieces clicked together.

"Who is he working for?" James asked, the hairs on his arms standing up, already anticipating her answer.

"Pavel Sokolov."

11

KYOJI TOHMATSU

One name charged the energy in the room and Kyoji didn't understand why. James's reaction didn't give it away—he was impossible to read. However, a barely audible, yet sharp intake of breath from the man next to him told a very different story.

Who is Pavel Sokolov?

Kyoji observed what happened next very carefully.

James rolled his lips over one another—thoughtfully, perhaps. And then he checked his watch.

"Why did Tanaka go rogue?" James asked.

Another pause.

When Angela answered, Kyoji thought he heard weariness in her voice.

"I don't know for sure, but apparently Tanaka's been playing both sides of the game. I believe he knew about the mission, Liam. He knew what the CIA intended to do when they sent you in. Apparently, after you started your revenge attacks, he decided it was safer to side with the Russians."

What the fuck had James Thomas done?

Whatever it was, Kyoji intended to find out more. If a man like this was in Tokyo, potentially running on his turf, it was his duty to find out. And make him a friend, Kyoji concluded. James was someone he wanted on his side.

Each drip of information was a tease, and it made this better than any soap opera Kyoji had ever seen.

"Is the CIA hunting him?" James asked, crossing his arms over his chest as he sat back in the chair.

"Of course they are. However, considering he's not retaliating against them, you're their primary focus."

"That's not why I'm their primary focus," James said, and Kyoji wondered what he meant by that.

Angela said nothing in response, and after a moment James continued. "Tanaka is as lethal as I am, and you know it."

"Potentially," Angela admitted. "But I'd put my money on you if there was a face-off. And it looks like there is."

Kyoji didn't know Tanaka other than their very brief meetings, but he'd put his money on James Thomas, too. There was something calculating about James—Kyoji saw it in his eyes—that Tanaka didn't have.

"If you want to survive," Angela said, "go. Get out of here. Hide—you know how to do it. Live a quiet life. Let this go now, you've done your part. It's finished."

"No, Ange," James said, looking at his brother, his expression inscrutable. "It's not finished."

12

JAMES THOMAS

It would never be finished. He'd never have a life where he didn't have to look over his shoulder. The day it finished was the day he died. And he didn't plan on seeing that day anytime soon.

James moved to the couch where his bag sat. He felt Ange's eyes on him. He pulled out another clear vial and a fresh syringe.

"Don't do this," she pleaded. "Please don't do this."

James nodded at Deacon and he stepped forward, grabbing her arms. She screamed, fighting back, but Deacon had her secured. Kyoji stepped in and bound the rope. Somehow they'd become a little team.

"I'm not going to hurt you," James said. "But I can't walk out of here and let you call a friend."

"I'm not going to talk, Liam. I give you my word." Her eyes begged as he kneeled in front of her.

"I don't know what your word is worth right now. But I'll know in twenty-four hours. If you talk, believe that I will come back for you." It was cold, harsh, but that's who he was. Ange didn't get a pass.

"I much prefer you in bed," Angela said. "You're less of an asshole."

James grinned, and then pierced the needle under her skin. She inhaled sharply. Their eyes locked, heated. "Goodnight, Ange."

The sedation worked fast—he'd given her a slightly higher dose than the one Kyoji had given her. She'd have a nice long sleep for a few hours or more; that would give them time to get out of Moscow before she potentially opened her mouth.

James brought his hand to her neck, supporting her head so it didn't slump forward.

"Cut her loose," James said to Deacon, and then he looked at Kyoji for the first time.

The man smirked. "Aren't you a bunch of fucking surprises?"

"Can you make yourself useful and grab her legs?" James asked, choosing not to respond to his comment. They needed to get on the road.

They lifted Ange onto the bed and James propped her up against the pillows, arranging them to keep her chest just slightly elevated.

He picked up her bag, which had been slung across her body, and searched through it, but he found nothing of interest. He did take her phone, though.

They turned off the lights, locked the door behind them, and stepped into the night.

"Where are we going?" Deacon asked as he put the car in reverse.

"We need to get out of Russia—now," James said, his hand on his pistol, his eyes bouncing between the mirrors.

The fact that Pavel Sokolov had gotten that close to him worried him more than the CIA finding him.

"We need to stop Tanaka before he returns to Tokyo. He will come back," James said, voicing his thoughts, trying to organize them.

The buildings blurred by so quickly they formed one continuous streak of white. Deacon wasn't wasting any time.

James needed a plan, and he needed it before they arrived back in Belarus.

"Does someone else in Tokyo know who you are?" Kyoji asked from the backseat.

James didn't think so, but if that was the case—Tanaka had the answer.

Finding Tanaka was now their focus.

After they cleared the outskirts of Moscow, James's eyes began to bounce between the mirrors every five seconds instead of every two.

"I need to draw Tanaka to me. Create a scene somewhere . . . It will throw them off Tokyo, and it will give me an opportunity to make Tanaka talk," James said, and then added, "if I can get him." Doubt hung in his mind. Tanaka was skilled, and James could easily end up dead.

But pulling a stunt like that could also alert the CIA, and then they'd all know where he was. James chances weren't good, but he wasn't going to wait for trouble to come to him, either. He'd never dealt with things that way. He faced things head on.

"Let's go to Cape Town," James said. In a city infiltrated by Russia, it'd be easy to get Sokolov's attention. James had spent time in the city as an agent, and he knew it well. If he was going to trap Tanaka, his chances were better there than anywhere.

James checked the mirrors again, seeing only darkness. He turned to Kyoji. "You can take the jet home from Polotsk—"

"Not a fucking chance," Kyoji said, shaking his head. "I'm going to Cape Town with you."

"The favor's done, Kyoji. You did your part," James said.

"I'm going with you, and let me tell you why. First, you're up to your neck in shit, and if I want any chance of redeeming this favor it'll help if you've got an extra set of hands to back you up."

"And second?" James asked, arching a brow.

Kyoji gave a sly smile. "I think it's in my best interest to learn as much about you as possible."

James didn't need to look at Deacon to know that his brother wasn't smiling.

An extra man in their corner could be a good thing, though. Especially one who wasn't adverse to violence—because if they did manage to capture Tanaka, he wasn't going to talk easily, and things would get ugly fast. Beyond that, Kyoji had a lot of something they didn't have—something that could be very handy in a city where bribery was rife: money.

~

Kyoji had arranged their flight details on the drive out of Russia and the jet had been ready to take off the moment they'd walked on. Having a private plane definitely made things easier.

Kyoji poured three glasses of whiskey as they sailed through the sky.

James permitted himself only a few mouthfuls. He needed a clear mind, one capable of strategizing. He took his first sip, letting the room-temperature liquid slide down the back of his throat, leaving a trail of heat.

James put his glass on the table, twisting it by the rim.

He looked at his companions, holding back his smile. Their appearances couldn't be more of a contrast—it was pretty boy versus Asian gangster.

"So, who is Pavel Sokolov?" Kyoji asked.

"He's the new head of the Russian mafia," James said with a sigh.

"*New* . . . because you slaughtered the men above him?" Kyoji asked.

"I don't think he wants to thank me for the promotion," James said.

Kyoji snorted, and then his eyes flickered to the right before coming back to James's. "Why did you spare him?"

"Not by choice." James grimaced. "We couldn't get to him—he's very well protected. We made a choice to leave and hope he never found us," James said.

James had only agreed to leave because he'd thought that they— he, Deacon, and Nicole—had a better chance of surviving if they did. Hiding three people together was hard. Hiding alone was much easier.

But now James wondered if they should've stayed in Russia and finished what they'd started. He dismissed it quickly, though, and returned his thoughts to the present—they'd made the choice, and now they had to deal with the potential consequences of it.

"We need to draw Sokolov's attention without involving Tanaka," Deacon said. "If Tanaka's doing his legwork now, Sokolov will send him. That part of the equation should take care of itself."

"Agreed," James said, taking his second—and final, he told himself—mouthful of his drink.

But how to draw Sokolov's attention?

The easiest way would be to walk into one of the nightclubs that Sokolov owned. But the men at the doors carried AK-47s, and things could turn bad fast. Especially because James would have to walk through a metal detector to enter, and that meant he couldn't take a pistol in.

"I need to make it look like a slip up," James said. "It will also benefit us if Tanaka thinks that we don't know we're being followed. We need to hold as many cards as possible."

He stared into his drink, looking for answers in the swirling amber liquid.

He didn't find it before his cell phone vibrated.

When he looked at the number, he knew bad news was on the way.

"Saito," James said.

"I've had a change of plans. I need you to attend a series of meetings tomorrow. I'll stay in the city for the rest of the week—there's no point going back to the farmhouse."

James cringed internally. He could tell Saito that they were out of town, but the man wouldn't be pleased, and he was volatile—he'd likely cancel the contract. A contract that paid extremely well and was relatively easy money. A contract they wanted to keep long-term.

There was really only one option.

James checked his watch, calculating the time zones. Deacon could get there in time—provided Kyoji let him use the jet.

"What time do you need one of us?" James asked.

"Midday will do."

"Deacon will be there," James said, looking at his brother.

"Excellent. I appreciate it."

James hung up. "He's had a change of schedule. He needs one of us there. You go to Tokyo, and I'll stay in Cape Town with Kyoji."

Deacon sighed. James knew he didn't like the plan, but he also knew the Saito contract was important.

"Tell Saito to fuck off," Kyoji said. "You can work for anyone, I'm sure."

"It's a good contract for many reasons," James said, not wanting nor needing to explain further.

Deacon nodded. "What time does he want me there?"

"Midday," James said.

Deacon looked thoughtful, and then whistled. "That's going to be tight."

James glanced at Kyoji. "Not if he loans you the jet."

Kyoji seemed to mull it over. "Okay . . . but I want something in return."

James should've known that was coming.

Kyoji continued. "I want your address in Tokyo. I want to know where to find you, if I should ever need to."

"Are you blackmailing us?" James asked, raising an eyebrow.

"No, I'm making a deal. This isn't the Boy Scouts, Thomas."

"Fine," James said, rolling his eyes. He'd give Kyoji their address —the one for the property they rented, but didn't actually live in.

"You've got a deal then, brothers," Kyoji said as he slid out from the table and moved toward the cockpit.

"It'll be all right," James said, reading his brother's thoughts. "I'll have Kyoji to back me up . . . what could possibly go wrong?" James cracked a joke to lighten the mood.

Deacon gave a sigh that bordered on a groan as he rubbed his eyes.

Kyoji returned. "All good. So, what's the plan for Cape Town, partner?"

They had limited time, and there was one method that made things happen faster than anything else.

The corner of James's lips turned up. "Extortion."

13

KYOJI TOHMATSU

Clouds cascaded over Table Mountain like rapid falls. It was picturesque, but Kyoji would've been just as happy to see it on a postcard from James Thomas.

He closed the gate behind him and lit a cigarette as he walked up the steep hill. James had secured an apartment that didn't risk bedbugs—something Kyoji was grateful for, bearing in mind how things had been in Russia—and they had it booked for two nights. They hoped they wouldn't need it any longer than that. Regardless, Kyoji had to make a call.

"How are things?" Haruki said, his tone cool.

"Complicated," Kyoji answered. He didn't want to give any details over the phone—he couldn't be sure how secure his line was. Being associated with James Thomas was not something he wanted the CIA to be aware of.

"That's very vague, son."

"I know. You have to continue to trust me on this one. The minute I get back, I'll meet you in your office. It's best we talk there."

Kyoji imagined his uncle sitting behind his large desk, his lips tight. Haruki was a man of few words, but those words could—and often did—kill.

"So why are you calling me?" Haruki asked.

"Because I'm going to be away a few days longer than expected. I have everything covered at the clubs. How things go depend on the next twenty-four hours. I'll keep you updated," Kyoji said, holding his breath.

A pause.

"I don't like this, but it's too late now, isn't it?" Haruki asked.

Far too late. "Trust me," Kyoji said.

He'd never let his uncle down, and he wouldn't start now.

"You have seventy-two hours, Kyoji. And then I want you back in Tokyo. This is not our fight," Haruki said.

"I'll be in touch," Kyoji said.

It wasn't their fight yet, but it could be if it came to Tokyo.

He turned on his heels.

It was time to play.

∼

The chair scraped against the concrete as Kyoji pulled it out, taking a seat. The white columns of the oceanfront bar were more European than African, Kyoji thought, but he'd never been to Africa. The images of sandy deserts and roaring lions were surely exclusive to a safari experience, which he didn't intend on having. He supposed, though, they were going to meet some lions of a different kind.

Kyoji looked at his apparent drinking companion, who was sporting a baseball cap and dark aviators. *I wouldn't recognize him if I didn't already know him.*

A waiter approached them, and James ordered two sodas. Kyoji rolled his eyes.

"Pass me your cigarettes," James said under his breath.

Kyoji slid them across the table, watching as James removed the lighter from the packet, sliding it into his pocket. He turned to the women sitting at the table behind them.

"Hey," James said, "do any of you have a light?"

His voice dripped with charm, and Kyoji grinned. James Thomas was a player when he wanted to be.

Two women grabbed for their handbags like it was a race and James was the prize. The other women looked disappointed—Kyoji assumed they weren't smokers and couldn't enter the competition.

The woman in the red dress won. She rolled her thumb over the flint and James leaned in, lighting the stick between his fingers. "Thanks," he said. "I owe you. So, are you from around here?"

Kyoji watched the scene play out in front of him and soon realized that none of it was accidental. As Kyoji was beginning to learn, James Thomas did everything with purpose. James had chosen this bar for a reason. He'd chosen the women seated at the table for a reason, and it wasn't so he could flirt with them—it was because their accents were strong. James knew they were locals before he'd even asked the question.

"We just flew in," James said. "We're here for a few days on business. Tell me"—James pointed to the mountain behind him—"whose house is that? It's like a palace."

The woman in red leaned forward, her arms accidentally—or not —pushing her breasts together. "Lev Ivanov," she said, her voice a throaty whisper. "You know, one of the Russians."

Kyoji got the sense that James already knew that, too. Or perhaps he'd had a hunch and had wanted to confirm it.

"Russian, huh?" James asked, keeping his voice low. "I did hear that they own a lot of businesses in the city now."

"A lot?" She smirked. "They own everything. Very powerful men."

"What about the Russian women?" James asked.

She puckered her lips, and then whispered. "Well, I don't think Mrs. Ivanov is a fool, but rather she turns a blind eye to what her husband's doing and where the money comes from. She lives in her castle, raises their three young children—with a lot of help—and lives a very expensive life. She seems happy enough."

"Good for her," James said. When the woman melted, Kyoji assumed James had flashed her a dazzling smile. "Well, thanks for the light," James said before he turned his back to them.

The women looked at Kyoji for the first time, and he made a note to never go to a bar with James Thomas if he wanted a pickup—he'd only get the seconds.

A ghost of a smile graced James's lips. "It's work, Kyoji," he said.

Kyoji scoffed. "Give me my fucking cigarettes."

James disappeared into the darkness, and Kyoji kept his back pressed against the fence—as instructed. His fingers tingled, and again he questioned if this was all worth it. Pissing off the Russian mafia was a very bad idea, and yet he couldn't shake the feeling that he'd need James in the future. Every time Kyoji opened his mouth to tell James to forget it—that he was on his own, that Kyoji was going back to Tokyo—the words escaped him and he closed his mouth again.

A twig snapped and Kyoji's heart lurched. His finger pulsed on the trigger—then James emerged from the shadows, and Kyoji let out a shaky breath.

"I just about fucking shot you," Kyoji whispered.

James grinned. "That would've been unfortunate. Come on, this way."

James walked back in the direction he'd just come from and Kyoji followed, his feet ignoring the voices in his head telling him to leave while he could.

"Up here," James said. "Use your fingertips to swing your legs up. The fence isn't electric." James crouched down and then launched up onto the concrete wall.

Kyoji cursed and then followed James's example.

He grunted as he catapulted his body. He took a second to catch his breath. When he did, he looked up and realized they were on the neighboring fence of the Ivanov residence.

Without saying a word, James pointed to six men, all carrying automatic weapons, pacing around the house.

"And you want to go in here?" Kyoji whispered, leaning in to hear the answer.

"No, we're not going to extort the big fish. He's got too much power and too much security."

"So, who *are* we going to extort then?"

"One of his men," James said as the property gates opened. "Wait here."

James managed to move along the walk with a speed that Kyoji found impressive, especially since he was bent over, keeping as low as possible.

A car entered the property, pulling to a stop in front of the house. A tall figure emerged from the front door, but Kyoji's view was partly blocked by two large trees.

A faint echo of voices floated through the night. Kyoji couldn't make out the words, but he didn't know if it was because the echo was so faint, or if they were speaking Russian.

Kyoji's eyes tracked to the wall where James sat, hidden by the shadows of the tree.

Suddenly, James turned and sprinted along the top of the wall.

Kyoji's pulse spiked.

"Go, go!" James hissed, jumping down to the ground, landing on all fours like a cat. He started sprinting in the direction they'd originally come.

Kyoji jumped.

14

JAMES THOMAS

Their black sedan sat like a phantom on the dark street and James sprinted toward it.

"Drive!" James shouted as he unlocked the car, jumping into the passenger seat.

Kyoji was a few seconds behind and James hoped like hell the guy could actually drive. James never drove because he was a better shot than a driver, and he couldn't effectively drive and shoot at the same time. James wished Deacon were behind the wheel, but he couldn't waste another second on wishful thinking right now.

"Head down to the water," James said and Kyoji did a U-turn while James loaded the navigation system on his phone.

"Do you want to tell me what the fuck is going on?" Kyoji asked.

"The guy that visited picked up a parcel. He's going to do a drop. We'll get him before he does it," James said. "Take the next right."

James had picked up the location through their conversation, and he had the license plate memorized. The next step would be the challenge.

James saw the car ahead, using his binoculars to identify the plates. It was a match. He looked at the map again. It was a risk, but they needed to take risks right now. Calculated risks.

"Okay, stay this distance behind him for two more blocks. We'll come up to a bend—push him to the exit. Hit his car if you need to. I'll take care of the rest," James said, already loading a second weapon.

He surveyed the road ahead. The cars were few and far between, which would work in their favor.

"Next block," James said, taking his eyes off his intended victim's car only to steal a look at Kyoji. He appeared to be in control. James was aware that although Kyoji rarely played by the rules, he had a level of control and comfort in Tokyo. He didn't have that here, and that had to have some effect on his mental state. He wasn't used to being thrown out into the wild.

"Increase your speed," James said, lowering his window. "Get alongside him now."

Kyoji kept the car steady, veering smoothly across the lanes. So far his driving skills were maintaining.

"Three, two, one!" James shouted and Kyoji turned the wheel hard, bumping the Russian's car, sending it veering toward the exit.

The Russian pulled it back, and James jolted from the impact.

"Push him!" James shouted, firing a shot at the Russian's wheel.

It hit and the car spun out of control, smashing into the road barrier.

"Stop!" James yelled and jumped from the car even before Kyoji had brought it to a complete stop.

The Russian was out of the car, his eyes wild. He brought up his pistol but James fired first, landing one in the arm.

The man screamed, dropping his weapon then scrambling to pick it up. James landed a knee to his chest, winding the man before he jammed a needle in his neck. It would've been easier to knock him out via physical means, but the method of sedation and reversal gave James more control over the timing of the Russian's return to consciousness.

A rant of Russian obscenities followed, but James was already dragging him back to their car as the man began to sway. James hauled him in just as the man's legs gave out.

"Go!" James shouted, and Kyoji pressed the accelerator to the floor.

"Where am I going?" he yelled with a hint of panic.

With the Russian slumped against the door, James drew his phone, making sure he gave Kyoji the correct directions.

He was going back to his old stomping grounds.

"Go straight through the next three intersections. At the fourth, take the first left, and then go left again," James said, kneeling on the back seat, his body humming, every nerve alive. He missed being an agent, he missed his old life.

Kyoji flew through the intersections as James's eyes darted. He watched everything—the other cars on the street, the pedestrians, the length of the lights. Years of experience had trained his mind to take in stimuli from multiple sources and create a picture with more clarity than a photograph. He hadn't been born with an eidetic memory, but he'd developed one that wasn't all that different.

Kyoji took a hard left, his foot not seeming to lift off of the accelerator.

"Slow down now," James said as they entered residential territory.

He'd wanted Kyoji to get as far away from the scene as possible, but now the goal was to attract as little attention as possible.

James checked the navigation system again, but his memory had served him well.

"See that bridge?" James said, leaning between the two front seats. "There's a lane just to the left. It'll take you through the park—keep veering right. I'll tell you when to stop. Dim your lights."

"Where are we?" Kyoji said as he peered forward, straining to see the road.

"Somewhere you shouldn't come without a pistol," James said, and he wasn't lying.

"Pull over here," James said. "I'll be back in a second."

Kyoji's eyes widened as if he were a little boy afraid of the dark. James didn't blame him—if the situation had been reversed, he wouldn't have trusted Kyoji either.

James jogged down the hill, exhaling in relief when he reached a set of steps. His memory hadn't just served him well—it had served him perfectly. He ran back to the car and stuck his head through the window, grabbing his kit. "Let's take our friend for a walk."

James grabbed the Russian by one arm, and Kyoji grabbed him by the other. The man's feet dragged as they pulled him down the bank, giving little care to any injuries the Russian might sustain in the process. But when they got to the stairs James knew the fastest way to move him would be to lift the heavy bastard.

James pulled a flashlight from his kit.

"On the count of three," James said, and Kyoji grunted as they bore the man's weight. They descended the stairs one by one. James led them deep into the tunnel.

"Stop here," James said, his chest heaving.

He gave them a minute to catch their breath but nothing more. They needed to do this quickly because their friend was supposed to make the drop in an hour, and he had a call to make before then.

"Drop him here," James said. They lowered the man to the ground, propping his back up against the tunnel wall.

James shined the flashlight in a roaming arc, floor to ceiling, looking for the switch. He found it and flicked it on, hoping the system still worked. The dim lights flickered twice before they stayed on.

"Aren't you resourceful?" Kyoji said, his eyes burning with unasked questions.

"Survival breeds resourcefulness," James said, kneeling next to his kit. He drew a dose of reversal—a dose larger than required. He wanted the man awake. Now.

James strapped a tourniquet on the man's bicep, flicked his vein a few times, and then injected it. They then set about binding the man before the reversal took effect. Not that he'd be a match for either James or Kyoji, not right after waking up from sedation.

"Where did you learn to do that?" Kyoji asked.

"I taught myself, on my own arm. Practice makes perfect . . ." He put two fingers on the man's neck. "Wakey, wakey," James said, ignoring the impatience bridling in his veins. His eyes dropped to his wristwatch—they still had time.

Slowly, the man began to rouse. James brought his hand to the man's cheek, giving him a helping hand. The Russian's eyes sprung open, hazy and unfocused. His eyes rolled back in his head again.

James gave him another helping hand.

A low, guttural groan fell from the man's lips as he pushed through the mind fog.

When his eyes managed to focus, his pupils dilated, and James knew his assumptions had been correct—Sokolov had circulated Liam Smith's image to every contact, in every corner of the world.

"Oh, fuck," the man said, trying to shuffle backward before he realized he was bound. He looked to the ceiling of the tunnel, cursed, and then returned his gaze to James. "What do you want?"

"I want you to make a call to Lev Ivanov. You're going to tell him you stopped at a gas station on your way to the drop, and I walked straight past you," James said, folding his arms across his chest.

"And why the fuck would I do that?" the Russian asked with a rough, raspy throat.

The man likely had a dry mouth as a result of the drugs. James wasn't giving him anything. Instead, James gave a haunting smile, one he knew would be amplified by the yellow lighting, and revealed what he'd been holding in the palm of his hand.

A scalpel.

The man shook his head furiously.

James nodded. "You're going to die within the next twenty minutes. How you die is completely up to you."

"Yebat' tebya," the man spat at him.

Fuck you.

James moved so fast the man didn't see it, nor did he likely feel the scalpel slice him, but he definitely felt the sizzling fire it left burning on his cheek.

The man howled, bucking his arms, but he couldn't get loose.

"Still want to play this game?"

The Russian's jaw clenched so tight his entire face became a picture of fury.

"I'm going to hold the phone to your cheek, and you're going to tell him exactly what I tell you to. And you will make it sound believable." James paused. "My Russian is very good."

"So I've heard," the man said, jutting out his chin.

"If you say anything I don't like, I will spend the next twenty-four hours here slicing you open from head to toe. If you know anything about me, you know I always keep my word. And that, my friend, is a promise."

The man's chest heaved, his shirt stretching with each breath.

"Do we have an agreement?" James asked.

The man pressed his teeth into his bottom lip, drawing blood.

"You're wasting my time," James said, waving the scalpel in front of him.

"You have a deal," the man said with dark eyes.

James detailed exactly what he wanted the man to say, and then searched through the Russian's phone for Ivanov's number. He connected a listening device that would allow him to hear both ends of the conversation without putting the phone on speaker.

He held the phone to the man's right ear with one hand, and a scalpel to the man's left ear with the other.

James's body pulsed, adrenaline pumping, as he listened to the phone ring. When Ivanov answered, he held his breath.

"You're never going to believe it," the Russian said, his words fast and quick just like James had instructed. "I just saw him. I saw Liam Smith."

Ivanov was silent for a moment.

"What? Where? Are you sure?"

"Positive. I just stopped at a gas station to refill, and he walked straight past me on his way out. It took me a second to register the face, and when I turned around he was gone—vanished. It was him, Ivanov. I've never been more sure of it."

"Good. Good. I'll deal with it. Continue onto the drop," Ivanov said, hanging up without a goodbye.

James couldn't be certain, but he thought Ivanov bought it. What happened now was crucial—they'd have to watch their backs at every turn, otherwise they could end up being the animals caught in the trap.

"Good," James said, giving his approval before pulling the listening device out of his ears.

The Russian looked at him with an odd expression—perhaps it was because he knew his death was imminent.

James drew his pistol, backed away a safe distance from the blood splatter, and fired three shots to the Russian's chest. The man's head wobbled before it slumped forward.

"Let's get out of here," James said without missing a beat, packing everything into his kit. He looked up when he felt Kyoji watching him.

"Problem?" James asked, raising one eyebrow.

Kyoji shrugged. "I wouldn't call it that," he said.

James opened his mouth to respond, but Kyoji beat him to it. "What are we going to do with him?"

"There's a compacting facility not far away," James said. It wasn't open to the public, but he doubted Bill would've forgotten his face.

Kyoji rubbed his jaw, and then said, "Good."

James wondered how much experience Kyoji had with disposing bodies. Probably a lot more in his earlier days, James concluded. He doubted Kyoji disposed any now, judging by the clean-up orders he'd seen him give in his club.

James laid out some black plastic sheeting, and they rolled up the Russian, securing him inside to protect the car from any blood. And then they set about the physically exhausting task of carrying the dead man back up the stairs—the one flaw of this location.

They shuffled back to the car and dropped the man in the truck. James leaned forward, resting his hands on his knees, panting. The man gave "deadweight" a new definition.

Kyoji slammed the trunk lid down. A thud followed, and it bounced back up.

"Oops," Kyoji said with a chuckle, shoving what James knew to be the man's head further inside the trunk.

James shook his head, but smiled despite himself.

The compacting yard was a good half-hour drive away and Kyoji drove carefully, monotonously—the last thing they wanted to do was draw attention right now.

They arrived without incident, and James dialed a number he hadn't used in a long time.

"Hawk," James said, giving the password.

"Bay six," a voice sounded from the speaker.

The gates opened and James guided Kyoji toward the concrete ramp.

"Stop here," James said, drawing an envelope from his kit.

Kyoji put the car in park, the idling engine the only noise cutting through the night. "What now?" Kyoji whispered, looking around.

Lights appeared behind them and James opened his door—stepping into the light, revealing his face.

The truck ignition ground to a halt, and the driver door swung open. The man's silver hair glimmered in the moonlight.

"Hey, Bill," James said, moving toward the man, offering him his hand.

"It's been a while, Agent Smith."

James nodded. "I've got one for you. He's in the trunk," James said, handing over the envelope.

Bill's smile stretched his face. "Consider it done."

15

KYOJI TOHMATSU

Kyoji rolled over, blinking as he focused on the neon lights. It was nearly midday.

He rubbed the crust from his eyes as he swung his legs to the ground. He heard the sound of voices talking and assumed it was coming from the television in the lounge room. James Thomas was apparently awake.

Kyoji fumbled around, finding his phone stuck in the sheets. He scrolled through his messages and his missed calls. He returned only one of them.

"Jayce. How are you?" Kyoji asked, cradling the phone between one ear and his shoulder as he looked for some pants, assuming James wouldn't appreciate him walking around in his birthday suit.

"Hey. I'm good—just working on the restructuring deal. What's up? Are you back in Tokyo?" Jayce fired the questions without a pause.

"No, I'm still in London," Kyoji said. He'd lied to Jayce about where he was going, for multiple good reasons—least of which was that he didn't want to worry him. "The negotiation is taking longer than I expected. I'll be home in a few days."

Jayce was under the impression Kyoji was negotiating a deal for a new business.

"Do you still think it's worth pursuing?" Jayce asked, a fitting question for the thoughts in Kyoji's mind.

"Long-term: yes." Even as Kyoji said the words, that nagging voice popped up, screaming at him to go home. But he didn't.

From what Kyoji had seen, James would've been one hell of an agent. So what did the CIA do that had made him turn his back and retaliate? That was the question Kyoji wanted the answer to. And he thought Tanaka had that answer.

James Thomas was a deadly man—one who Kyoji intended to stay on the right side of—but if he ever caused trouble in Tokyo, Kyoji wanted to know everything about him. Knowledge was power.

"Anyway, I'd better go," Kyoji said, desperately wanting a shower.

"Why so quick, brother? Do I even want to know who you've got in your bed?"

Kyoji chuckled as he cast his eyes upon his crumpled, barren sheets. "You won't believe this, but I haven't had any pussy for days now."

Jayce scoffed. "No, I don't believe that."

"It's true," Kyoji said. James was a real cockblocker. "I'll talk to you soon, Jayce. Take care. Call me if you need anything."

"Sure. Good luck with the deal," Jayce said and hung up.

Kyoji sighed, looking at the bed once more. He rolled his eyes and got in the shower. The sooner he got home the better—for many reasons.

James sat at the dining table eating a bowl of cereal and watching the news. A complete contrast to the man of action he had been last night.

Kyoji joined him, pleased to see there was also a pot of coffee on the table. He poured himself a cup and took in a mouthful. His face twisted as it burned the back of his throat. Kyoji wondered if they'd be going out today, somewhere he could get real coffee, but he already knew that they weren't leaving the safety of their apartment until James had a plan. All of the Russians were looking for him, and apparently that meant half the city was—the half that should be feared.

"How'd you sleep?" James asked.

Kyoji rubbed the crick out of his neck. "Good. Except for that pillow . . ."

James gave him a lopsided grin.

"What?" Kyoji asked.

"You're very precious when it comes to accommodation."

"Precious? Just because I want a pillow that isn't paper-thin?"

James chuckled. "You don't know how lucky you are," he said with faraway eyes. He shook his head, seeming to return to the present moment.

"I think you're a man of many secrets and many names, James Thomas," Kyoji said, gulping another mouthful as if he were drinking medicinal syrup. He just wanted the caffeine hit.

"I think you have plenty of your own secrets, Kyoji," James said pointedly.

Kyoji ignored the remark. "What does all of this achieve?" Kyoji asked. "Even if you kill Tanaka . . . you can't escape your past. It will always be in your shadow. Why not just leave Tokyo and keep running?"

"I'm not trying to escape the past," James said. "I'm trying to provide some stability. We'll have to run for the rest of our lives, but if we can stay in one place for a few years . . . well, that's a totally different ballgame. Constantly running is mentally taxing."

Kyoji eyeballed him, wondering if he should dare to ask the question. "For you or your brother?"

"Both," James said without a moment of hesitation, without a flicker of conflict in his eyes. Still, Kyoji didn't believe him.

He changed the subject. "So, what is the plan for today?"

James consumed the last spoonful of his cereal and then pushed the bowl away. "We need to give Tanaka a few hours to get here—

assuming that's who Sokolov will send, and I'm almost sure he will be. Tanaka went to Paris from Tokyo, but he's the kind of man who wouldn't stay in one place long, so he could've been anywhere in the world last night. I'm thinking"—he paused, casting his eyes down on at his wrist—"that we wait another six hours to set the plan in motion. That'll take us to sunset, and I prefer to move about in the dark."

"Okay," Kyoji said. "But how exactly are we going to capture only Tanaka's attention and not the rest of the city's? I would prefer to keep my involvement hidden from the Russians."

James gave an award-winning smile. "I've got an idea. One that might just be my best yet."

~

The sky transformed before their eyes. Orange and yellow ribbons faded into cobalt streaks and the wispy clouds hung to the mountain like cobwebs.

Kyoji kept his eyes ahead, lifting his foot off the accelerator as another tight corner emerged. Kyoji was tense enough driving up the mountain at dusk—but coming down, in the black depths of the night, would be heart-palpitating.

Let's hope we will be coming down the mountain.

His eyes dropped to the cell phone on the center console of the car. The Russian's cell phone. They'd turned it off and taken out the battery last night—effectively disconnecting it so they couldn't be tracked. But now the battery was in, the phone was on, and they were sending a trail of breadcrumbs they hoped the Russians were going to follow.

When James had detailed the plan over more bad coffee and a second box of cereal, Kyoji was impressed to say the least. *Stunned* was perhaps the better word. And he learned one more thing about James Thomas: he was a tactician above all.

There was a reason two men—James and Deacon Thomas—had been able to obliterate the most powerful men of the Russian mafia, with seemingly few resources, and no backup: skilled, masterful planning.

James Thomas was the ultimate player. The ultimate strategist. One Kyoji intended to make a very good friend.

"Pull up here," James said, pointing to a small, wooden gazebo.

Kyoji turned off the ignition and exhaled a silent breath. He got out of the car, stretching his arms up to the heavens as he looked down on the glittering lights of Cape Town. Kyoji wasn't sure how high up they were, but he wondered if he'd ever been closer to heaven. Not that he actually thought he'd be allowed entry—if such a place even existed. He doubted James would be getting in either. *Although James would probably find a way to break in and scare the fuck out of God.* Kyoji smiled, and James looked to him. "What?"

Kyoji shook his head. "Nothing."

James looked puzzled but then seemed to let it go. They had things to do, and in a few minutes Kyoji doubted he'd be able to see his own feet. Not to mention, the Russians were likely already on their way.

James moved in long strides toward the gazebo. He put his kit down on the cement, pulling out various items. Kyoji watched with interest, like he always did. Nothing the brothers had—that Kyoji had seen, anyway—was particularly advanced or technical. James's earlier comment came back to him: if Kyoji wanted sophisticated gadgets, he should go work for the CIA. The resources James had available to him now must've been a dramatic downgrade from what he'd previously worked with, but it didn't seem to bother him. He appeared to take advantage of whatever was available without complaint. In fact, Kyoji didn't think he'd heard him complain once. Not about anything. And from what Kyoji had learned, he had more than a few reasons to complain.

"Hold this," James said, and Kyoji took the light from his hands, holding it over him. James connected several wires to the Russian's phone, inserted an earpiece into his ear, and then appeared to test the phone. "Good," James muttered and then grabbed a roll of electrical tape, securing the wires around the phone. He then taped the phone to the underneath of the bench seat in the gazebo.

"Part one done," James said, picking up his kit bag and slinging it over his shoulder. "Five parts to go."

Kyoji snorted as James patted him on the shoulder as he walked by, sliding into the passenger seat.

Kyoji reversed up, careful not to go over the edge of the mountain, and then turned back onto the road.

"Through there," James said, his voice calm. No hint of trepidation. No hint of fear. No hint of panic. He spoke as if it were an ordinary day in the office.

Kyoji steered the car onto the thin, narrow dirt road that Kyoji would've missed had James not pointed it out.

"Turn the lights off," James said.

Without the lights on, Kyoji lifted his foot off of the accelerator, letting the car roll along, easing it into the tunnel.

"Are you sure we're not driving toward the edge of the mountain?" Kyoji asked. He couldn't see more than a few meters in front of him, and that made his spine tingle.

"Positive. This tunnel goes straight through the tip of the mountain."

"Is that how we're getting to the other side?" Kyoji said.

"No," James said. "Park right here."

"Here?" Kyoji asked, flattening his foot on the brake. He looked around. They were smack in the middle of the tunnel.

James put a small black box on the dashboard.

"What's that?" Kyoji replied.

"Something I prepared while you were sleeping this morning," James said.

Interesting, Kyoji thought, taking another look at it.

James turned to him, wearing a grin just visible from glimmer of the full moon. "Let's have some fun."

16

JAMES THOMAS

The car was James's last resort—his backup if the plan failed. It still didn't mean they'd survive, but he hoped it would give them a fighting chance. If he did have to use it, though, it'd be a long walk down the mountain. Something he hadn't told Kyoji.

James noted the time on his watch as he took the first step away from the car. They wove through the trees but James didn't lift his eyes to take in the spectacular views of the city below. His mind was focused. He paused at the rocks, his head tilting backward. It was a short climb, no more than a few body-lengths, but it was an almost vertical shaft—something else he hadn't mentioned to Kyoji.

"You're fucking kidding me," Kyoji swore.

"Unfortunately not," James said, securing his kit across his chest. "I'll go up first." He ran his fingertips along the rock, looking for leverage. He found two small grooves, and then another few, climbing like Spiderman.

He grunted as his arms hauled the last of this weight, his knees finding the top of the shaft. He ran a light along the path that led to the other side of the mountain—it was thinner than he'd remembered, but he'd walked it this morning while Kyoji had been distracted with the explosives.

This section of the mountain curved like a horseshoe, and this path was the only access to the platform that was conveniently located across from the gazebo—a small canyon the only thing separating them.

James hoped the Russians didn't know about the path. He doubted they did. James only knew because on a stint here he'd used it for a similar setup, and it had taken him months of research and help from the local people.

"Come on up," James said, wondering what Kyoji's limits were. The path ahead might be one of them.

Kyoji mumbled something under his breath but followed James up the shaft. James extended a helping hand, pulling him up. Kyoji pressed his back against the mountain, his head turning side to side. "What the fuck?"

Whatever Kyoji had been expecting to see, he didn't find it. James pointed the flashlight down the path.

"No! No way! What is *wrong* with you?" Kyoji asked, pressing his hands against the mountain as if he were trying to push it back, to put some distance between himself and the path, or possibly himself and James.

"We can meet the Russians down by the car if you'd like," James said. "But our chances won't be good."

Kyoji peered around the mountain again. "There's no railing."

"Unfortunately not," James said with a grimace. "It widens up. It's just this first part that's a little rough."

"A little? I might as well be walking on a tight rope," he said.

"Are you scared of heights?" James asked.

"No. I just don't want to fall off the fucking mountain," Kyoji snarled as his head snapped in the direction of the gazebo.

James's ears pricked, his body still as he listened. He made out the faint hum of a warm engine—one climbing up the mountain—but it wouldn't be faint for long. And he doubted the car was alone.

Kyoji took a quick step toward him. When faced with the path or the Russians, it was an easy choice.

"Stay close. I'll go first," James said.

"Damn right you will. And if I fall, I'm taking you with me."

James grinned as he put one foot in front of the other, testing the path again, making sure he didn't slip. Luckily, Cape Town had had a whisper of rain in the last few days, and that meant that the ground was solid—not wet, but not dry. Perfect hiking conditions.

Kyoji's breath was heavy in his ear—a likely effect of nerves rather than exertion, given that the path was flat.

As the path began to widen, James felt the tension melt from his own body. They could walk side by side now, but Kyoji chose to stay a pace behind. James knew the side of his body was chafing against the mountain.

"We have to go back that way, don't we?" Kyoji asked as they came to the small platform.

"Yes," James said while pointing down. Kyoji's eyes followed his hand.

Four sets of headlights.

James crouched, assembling his rifle and double-checking it. Kyoji did the same.

Twenty men, James estimated, based on the number of cars. Twenty men against two. He'd faced worse odds.

Neither James nor Kyoji spoke as they watched the cars finish their ascent. Even the mountain was quiet. It was like the wildlife had known to clear out for the night or risk getting shot.

James looked through the lens of the sniper rifle, focusing on his breath, keeping it long and steady.

The SUVs stopped in front of the gazebo, forming an arc. Their high-beams lit up the sky.

Breathe.

Focus.

Men exited the cars as fluidly as an army of ants emerging from their nest. They were in full SWAT gear, their hands at shoulder height, weapons locked and loaded.

Eighteen men on the ground, James counted.

The men scoured the area only to regroup in the gazebo.

James dialed the Russian's phone, and he could hear its shrill ringing from where they were positioned.

The men reacted fast, cutting it loose.

"Who is in charge?" James asked.

"Who the fuck is this?"

"This is Liam Smith. Give the phone to whoever is in charge."

The Russian lowered the phone from his ear, and appeared to speak to the man next to him.

"What's he doing?" Kyoji asked, a hushed whisper.

"Relaying a message," James said.

Come on.

The man holding the phone moved toward one of the cars. The window rolled down, and the phone was passed in.

"Liam," a rough voice said.

"Are you in charge?" James asked.

"Yes."

"Step out of the car," James commanded, watching the response of the men in the gazebo. Their backs straightened, their heads sweeping as their eyes roamed.

As James had suspected, they were all wired.

"Why would I want to do that?"

James deepened his voice, adding an edge to his tone—it was a tone he'd perfected over the years. "Because if you don't, I'll activate the explosives buried underneath the very ground your car is parked on, and the ground your men are standing on. Get out of the car."

A beat passed. And then two.

James counted down from five. When he got to two, the door opened, and a man stepped out: Tanaka.

"Okay, Smith. I'm out of the car," Tanaka said.

Tanaka had one hand on the open car door—he was barely outside the vehicle.

"Walk into the gazebo. Into the center," James said.

Tanaka stood still for a pause, as if considering his next move, but then walked toward the gazebo.

"I'm inside the gazebo," Tanaka said.

James nodded at Kyoji, who held one of seven triggers in his hand.

A cracking roar was followed by a fiery ball of orange and yellow hues that lit up the mountain. The men reacted, scrambling backward, their heads darted side to side.

"Consider that a warning," James said as his eyes shot to the blaze already dying behind the cars. He'd intentionally set it near rock. He wanted Tanaka alive, not a charred crisp.

"Where are you, Smith?" There was venom in Tanaka's voice.

"Closer than you think. Step into the gazebo, count the fifth post from your right, and look up."

This time Tanaka did as commanded, looking straight into the camera.

"Oh, now I see you," James said.

Tanaka didn't smile.

"Tell your men to get out of the gazebo," James said, looking through the sniper lens even though the camera was active. He wanted to see the entire picture.

When no one moved, James nodded to Kyoji.

A second, rocketing explosion rattled the men. James could see the loss of confidence even from where he was. They were losing faith—they were starting to panic. They were on top of a mountain, on a protruding corner, and the only exit was blocked by explosives. They began to group in clusters, all backing toward the gazebo.

James and Kyoji had to move fast now. They'd already attracted far too much attention, but being on top of the mountain had one other advantage: it was at least a forty-five minute drive for law enforcement to get to them.

"Tell your men—" James didn't even have a chance to finish before Tanaka issued the command.

"Out of the gazebo. Move! Toward the cars!" Tanaka shouted, waving his arm in the direction of the vehicles.

James took the opportunity to zoom in on some of the men. Their eyes were wide.

"Is there anyone still in the cars?" James asked.

"No," Tanaka said, staring into the camera.

Kyoji blew up the car on the far right.

"Are you sure? This will be your last chance to save them."

"What are you doing, Liam? What game are you playing?" Tanaka said tensely, his eyes wild.

"Last chance," James warned.

Tanaka spun on his heels. "Get out!"

James shook his head, but stilled when he saw who exited: Lev Ivanov.

His wife would become a widow after all.

"I fucking hate being lied to," James said, ending the call.

Kyoji didn't even need a cue. The cars exploded one after the other like dominoes.

"Fucking Russians," Kyoji cursed as he dropped the triggers and went for his rifle instead.

James refocused, taking a steadying breath, aimed, and fired the shot. It hit Tanaka's foot. He couldn't hear Tanaka's howl over the crackling of the fiery blaze, but his contorted face confirmed the hit.

Tanaka crumpled to the floor and then crawled toward the edge of the gazebo. James took his eyes off him, only because he knew there was nowhere for Tanaka to go. He wouldn't be able to get past the wall of fire.

"Oh yeah," Kyoji said next to him, and James couldn't help the smile that formed on his lips. When he angled his rifle to Tanaka's men, he saw why Kyoji was so excited.

Half of them were already on the ground. James had tested Kyoji's performance with a rifle earlier, but apparently he performed even better under pressure.

James zoned in, his finger light on the trigger, his mind and body in perfect sync. He moved into the zone that had become his favorite place, and the world ceased to exist except for the scene in front of him.

One man fell after another. The fire was doing a brilliant job of keeping them contained. James homed in on one man scrambling toward the gazebo, his finger pulsing on the trigger, but he was a second too late—Kyoji's bullet hit him.

"Good night," Kyoji said. His ability to talk and shoot was remarkable.

James turned his rifle, scouting for any remaining men. The only one he saw moving was Tanaka.

James threw his rifle and phone into his bag. "Let's go!"

Kyoji jumped up and James heard his footsteps a stride behind. James sprinted along the path, slowing down when they reached the narrow ledge.

"Don't ever expect me to walk this path again, Thomas," Kyoji said.

James grinned but kept his attention on the ground beneath his feet. It would be a shame to slip off when Tanaka was putty in his hands.

"Thank fuck for that," Kyoji said as they reached the vertical shaft.

Going down was a lot easier than climbing up.

James jumped, landing in a crouched position. He waited for Kyoji to jump too, his arm outstretched to catch him if he somehow slipped and fell. When they were both safe on two feet, they ran through the shrubs, past the car, stopping only when they neared the gazebo. The fire was dying down but James still used the extinguisher they'd hidden earlier to clear a solid path. James went left, creeping up behind Tanaka. He pressed his pistol to Tanaka's temple.

"Put your weapon down," James ordered.

A sigh fell from Tanaka's lips. The gun dropped to the ground.

"I'll take that," Kyoji said, stepping in front of Tanaka, a wicked smile on his lips.

Kyoji scooped up the weapon from the ground, keeping his own pointed at Tanaka.

"You! You son a bitch!" Tanaka growled.

Kyoji smirked. "What can I say? I like to play on the winning team."

"Hello, old friend," James said, coming to crouch in front of Tanaka, their eyes level, their stares like darts.

James flicked his wrist, lowering his eyes for a split second. They had to move now. He drew a syringe from his pocket and Tanaka's eyes doubled in size.

"No! No!" Tanaka begged.

Kyoji stepped forward, pressing his pistol into Tanaka's chest. "Stay still," he said playfully.

Kyoji seemed to be enjoying himself.

James jammed the needle into Tanaka's neck.

17

KYOJI TOHMATSU

Kyoji's heart thumped against his chest, a heady mixture of adrenaline and exertion flowing through him. They dumped Tanaka in the backseat, and then Kyoji took the driver's position. He was not looking forward to driving down the mountain, but there was no way to go but down.

"You can use your high-beams. We should be safe for another fifteen minutes," James said, looking at his wrist.

Kyoji had a million questions to ask, some more important than others, but right now he had to concentrate on reversing without hitting a tree. When he got clear of the shrubs, he backed into a small opening, put the car in drive and put his foot down on the accelerator.

They could've continued through the tunnel and down the mountain, but James advised there were no roads leading off it until the bottom of the mountain. They could get trapped, so they were going down the way they'd come up. They just had to reach their intended exit point before they met the cops.

James had calculated it would take them ten minutes to reach it. That gave Kyoji a small window, and he intended to take full advantage.

He drove past the remnant flames still licking the rocks of the mountain. The police were going to have a mess to clean up when they arrived, but even Kyoji knew the media would never hear of the massacre—it wasn't good for tourism.

Kyoji relaxed his grip on the steering wheel when his hands began to cramp. He was conscious of the time, the tight corners, and of how heavily he was riding the brakes.

James was quiet, although that wasn't uncommon. He was often a man of few words, but Kyoji thought that inside his head was a very different story. Always alert, always watching, never negligent.

James's window was down, and the crisp air bit at Kyoji's skin.

"Can you put your window up? It's fucking freezing," he said.

"No, I need to listen," James responded.

For what? Kyoji thought, but he let it go as he swung the car around another corner.

"Just a few more minutes," James said.

Kyoji nodded, relieved.

And then he heard it, realizing what James had been listening for. Sirens sounding in the distance like a melody.

"How far?" Kyoji asked.

"Just drive," James said with a sense of urgency. "On your left, two hundred meters."

Kyoji resisted the urge to brake as they neared the bend—the sirens were growing louder, and they had to be off this road before the police saw their lights.

One wheel slid on the gravel as he took the corner sharp, sending his heart lurching, but he pulled the car back just as James yelled, "Here!"

Kyoji slammed on the brakes, realizing he couldn't make the turn.

He changed gears, sending the car backward, before he pulled it into drive, just making the corner.

"Keep going," James said, kneeling on the seat, looking out the rear window.

Kyoji didn't look behind them—he kept his eyes forward.

When James turned around, fastening his seat belt once again, Kyoji exhaled a long breath.

"Drive for another twenty minutes, then we'll pull over and wake up our friend," James said.

"You're going to do it here on the mountain?" Kyoji asked.

"I want to do it somewhere that no one will hear him scream."

~

Kyoji rubbed his arms to keep himself warm. James didn't appear affected by the frosty air at all, and Kyoji wondered if that was because he was running on adrenaline.

Tanaka was propped up against a rocky shaft, and James had given him the reversal a few minutes ago. His feet started twitching first, and then his body began to tremble. James crouched beside him, using a large rock as a table for the items he was unpacking. Kyoji was grateful he'd chosen Team Thomas.

Unlike the night before, James let Tanaka wake up on his own time without a helping hand to the cheek. Kyoji wondered why that was. Was it simply because they weren't under such tight time constraints?

Kyoji had strung two flashlights in the trees, providing ample lighting for James to do whatever it was he was going to do. Kyoji sat on the edge of the car seat, leaving the door wide open, giving him a perfect view of these one-time colleagues. Two rogue CIA agents. Stranger things had never happened to him.

"Wake up, Tanaka," James said, his voice strong and loud.

Tanaka groaned, opening and closing his eyes several times. When they did stay open, he squinted like the light was burning them

"Taking sides with Pavel Sokolov was your first mistake," James said. "Hunting me was your second."

James tapped a scalpel against the palm of his hand. He really loved that scalpel, which said a lot about him. Mentally speaking, if you planned to kill someone, it was easiest to fire a bullet; it was harder to stab someone. And then there was James—it took a special kind of person to enjoy slicing someone up. Kyoji knew this from experience.

"Joining Sokolov wouldn't have been a mistake if you hadn't fucked it all up," Tanaka said through clenched teeth.

"Me?" James asked, sounding genuinely surprised. "Please tell me how I did that."

"By asking questions you shouldn't have. You forced the CIA's hand. You gave them no option but to attempt to eliminate you."

"No option?" James questioned, his voice noticeably deeper. "I didn't ask to be sent into a bloodbath. I didn't ask to take two teams of men in—innocent, good men dedicated to serving their country—only so that the CIA could kill them off to protect their own interests."

Kyoji's spine tingled, sensing he was about to hear something big. Something a man like him should never know.

"Their blood is on your hands," Tanaka said, his voice like a growling dog's. "They died because *you* had to be taken out. They died because of you—because you uncovered the assassination plot."

"Their blood is not on my hands," James said, and Kyoji almost shrank back at the sound of his voice. It was nothing like the James Thomas he'd heard at any stage over the weekend. This was a different man—a vehement man.

"It is. You fucked everything. You fucked my life," Tanaka said, continuing to mouth off, digging himself deeper into hell.

"Your life? What the hell does this—?" James stopped suddenly, and Kyoji wished he could see his face.

James continued, speaking slowly now. "It was you. I could never work out how they were going to do it, but now it makes sense. You were the agent that was going to perform the assassination."

"That's right, I was," Tanaka said with a pissed-off smile. "That's why I was partnered with the Russians, and that's why I had to side with them after they failed to kill you. I was better protected with the Russians."

James stared long and hard at Tanaka.

"What the fuck did it matter to you?" Tanaka asked. "Why did you care if Kozlov died?"

Kozlov? Kyoji searched his brain, stilling when he realized who they were talking about. *Holy fuck.* Kozlov was the Russian president.

"I didn't. I cared why the mafia wanted to do that since they were supposed to be in bed with the Russian government. And I cared why the CIA was involved, and why they were so happy to expend agents' lives in the process."

"Agents' lives are expended all the time. So are those of military men," Tanaka said.

"Not when they're under my watch," James said. "Now . . ." He pressed the scalpel into the skin between Tanaka's eyebrows. "Tell me: who led you to Tokyo?"

Tanaka hissed in a breath as James turned the scalpel.

Goddamn. James was going to bore a hole in Tanaka's skull.

"Who led you to Tokyo?" James repeated.

Tanaka made a wailing noise as his chest wheezed. "I didn't know you were in Tokyo," he finally said.

James sighed, shaking his head. He twisted the scalpel again. Droplets of blood chased one another down Tanaka's nose, dripping from the tip.

"I didn't know!" Tanaka yelled. "We got a lead on South Korea. There's a guy doing contract work there . . . he fit your description. I went to check it out."

James twisted the scalpel a full turn. Tanaka screeched, his body shaking, his teeth crunching together.

"How did you end up in Tokyo?" James asked, his voice calm, controlled.

"My ex-girlfriend lives there," Tanaka said. "I thought I'd call in for a fuck and ask a few questions while I was there . . . at least make the trip productive. When you've been searching for someone for a year without a bite of success, you start getting desperate. Every city I've been to in the past six months I've asked questions. I had no idea when I left that you'd been right under my nose."

Tanaka's gaze turned to Kyoji.

His eyes were like ice, piercing a dagger through Kyoji's chest, but Kyoji didn't back down.

JAMES THOMAS

James's eyes flickered to Kyoji, who returned Tanaka's glare with a smile of a man who would not be intimidated.

"Look at me," James said, "or I'll cut your eyes out. It'll be the most painful thing you'll experience for the rest of your very short life."

Tanaka's chilling eyes landed on James once more.

Tanaka could've been so good. He could've done great things. Instead he had gotten greedy, willing to progress his career via any means possible—at any cost, humans not excluded. When men got greedy they fell—and it was a long way to fall from the top.

James flicked the scalpel, taking a chunk out of Tanaka's forehead. Blood bubbled before it gushed over his face and down his neck, soaking into his shirt.

"What other leads does Sokolov have? Where is he looking?" James asked.

"I told you! He doesn't have any! The CIA doesn't have any. No one can find you or the Ranger. You're like ghosts; walking on the earth, among the people, showing yourselves only when you want to. They. Have. Nothing."

James didn't think Tanaka was lying. And Angela's intel backed it up. In that case, Tanaka had just gotten lucky in Tokyo—depending on how you looked at it.

James leaned in, looking into the eyes of a dead man. "You were a good agent. It's just a shame you're such a weak man."

James slashed the scalpel across Tanaka's throat, and the man gulped for air like a dying fish.

James watched as he took his final breaths.

He could go back to Tokyo. They—their little family of three—could stay there, for a while at least. Until they had a reason to move, it was pointless to keep running. If Sokolov's men were asking about them in every city they went to, there was nowhere safe for them to hide. They could live remotely, but that presented a challenge—work. Contract work was plentiful in cities and like a drought in country towns. At some point they'd need to move on again; but for now, Tokyo was their home.

James turned to his new friend, and—hopefully—future ally.

"Are you just going to sit there, or are you going to help?" James asked, smirking.

"I'll help when you put that scalpel away," Kyoji said with a chuckle. He didn't make a move until James had cleaned it and packed it back in his kit.

Kyoji joined him, looking at Tanaka's bloody body. "Is he going to the compacting yard, too?"

James nodded.

"Business has been good for Bill this week," Kyoji joked.

James peered out of the window, casting his eyes down. The lights of Tokyo blossomed together like a constellation. He'd called Deacon the moment they'd boarded the plane. To say he sounded relieved was an understatement, and James knew Nicole would feel the same way. Looking at the city they called home, James wondered if he'd ever truly think of Tokyo as home. He'd never really thought of anywhere as home.

"There's no place like Tokyo," Kyoji said, pride in his voice.

James smiled. "Do you think you'll ever live anywhere else?"

"Maybe," Kyoji said. "Business opportunities are everywhere. But Tokyo will always be home, and I'll never be gone for too long."

Kyoji looked back to James. "What happens for you now—other than doing my security fit-outs, I mean?"

James grinned. "We'll continue doing Saito's detail and take things one day at a time. Maybe one day we'll grow it into a full-fledged security company." James held Kyoji's gaze. "Thank you. You took a chance on us. I wasn't really expecting you to say yes."

Kyoji nodded, a small smile on his lips. "I'll keep my ears open for you. If I hear anything at all, I'll pass it on."

"I appreciate that," James said. He might not have made a friend, but he had an ally in Kyoji, and that was better for a man like himself.

Kyoji tapped his fingertips on the table, an odd look in his eyes. "I think your story is a long way from over, isn't it?"

James thought about that for a moment. "Given my past, anything is possible."

//

HUNGRY FOR MORE?

The fist novel of Deacon Thomas' spin-off series will be released in September 2017.

In the meantime, you can catch up with the characters again in *The Soul Series*.

I'm giving away the first book of this series, *The Secrets of Their Souls*, for **FREE**. All you need to do is sign up at http://brookesivendra.com/tsots-download/

Enjoy!
Brooke

ALSO BY BROOKE SIVENDRA

THE SOUL SERIES

The Secrets of Their Souls (Book One)

The Ghosts of Their Pasts (Book Two)

The Blood of Their Sins (Book Three)

The Soul Series Box Set (Books One - Three)

DID YOU ENJOY THIS BOOK?

As a writer, it is critically important to get reviews.

Why?

You probably weigh reviews highly when making a decision whether to try a new author—I definitely do.

So, if you've enjoyed this book, and would love to spread the word, I would be so grateful if you could leave an honest review (as short or as long as you like) on Amazon.com.

Thank you so much, Bx

ABOUT THE AUTHOR

Brooke Sivendra lives in Adelaide, Australia with her husband and two furry children—Milly, a Rhodesian Ridgeback, and Lara, a massive Great Dane who is fifty pounds heavier than Brooke and thinks she is a lap dog!

Brooke has a degree in Nuclear Medicine and worked in the field of medical research before launching her first business at the age of twenty-six. This business grew to be Australia's premier online shopping directory before Brooke sold it to focus on her writing.

You can connect with Brooke at any of the channels listed below and she personally responds to every comment and email.

www.brookesivendra.com
brooke@brookesivendra.com
Facebook: www.facebook.com/bsivendra
Twitter: www.twitter.com/brookesivendra
Instagram: www.instagram.com/brookesivendra

Cover by Virtually Possible Designs

Ebook: 978-0-6480649-4-7

Print: 978-0-6480649-5-4

Made in the USA
Middletown, DE
01 October 2018